My Husband's Mistress Is Me

My Husband's Mistress Is Me

R. Simone

www.urbanbooks.net

Urban Books, LLC
300 Farmingdale Road, NY-Route 109
Farmingdale, NY 11735

My Husband's Mistress Is Me

ISBN 13: 978-1-64556-183-5
ISBN 10: 1-64556-183-6

First Trade Paperback Printing February 2021
Printed in the United States of America

10 9 8 7 6 5 4 3 2 1

This is a work of fiction. Any references or similarities to actual events, real people, living or dead, or to real locales are intended to give the novel a sense of reality. Any similarity in other names, characters, places, and incidents is entirely coincidental.

Distributed by Kensington Publishing Corp.
Submit Orders to:
Customer Service
400 Hahn Road
Westminster, MD 21157-4627
Phone: 1-800-733-3000
Fax: 1-800-659-2436

My Husband's Mistress Is Me

by

R. Simone

To my loving and supportive family, my true and everlasting friends, my "secret" reviewers who helped me perfect my work of art, and last but not least, all the people who said this couldn't be . . .

This one's for you.

Forever grateful,

—R. Simone

P.S. Continue to rest in peace, Daddy. I love you, and I hope that I am making you proud.

In Loving Memory of Ronald S. Pleasant
September 19, 1951 to August 24, 1995

Introduction

"Wow, what a day!" Rene mumbled to herself as she tucked her books into her backpack. Her last final was the next day, and she would finally be done with school. It had taken her eight long years to complete her bachelor's and master's degrees, but it was all worth it. She had a $150,000-a-year job waiting for her, with a loving husband and two beautiful children to share it with.

As Rene walked the pathway back to the parking garage, she began to think of how fortunate she was to have so many people in her life who loved her. Not only did she have her family, but she also had an amazing best friend. A best friend who was willing to do anything to make sure she was successful.

"Hello," answered Rene.

"Hey, baby! How you doing?" asked the chipper and energetic voice on the other end of the phone.

Rene smiled. "Hey, Mama. I'm doing okay. My brain hurts, but I'm okay."

"Your brain hurts?" asked Ms. Martha, Rene's mother. "How on earth does that happen?"

Rene shook her head and smiled. Her poor mother could be very simple at times. "I just finished my study session for my last final. My brain hurts because I've been thinking too hard," she explained.

Ms. Martha let out a loud laugh. "Okay, okay. I getcha now! I actually was calling to speak to my grandbabies. I feel like I haven't seen them in a month."

Ms. Martha was not only simple at times, but a bit of an exaggerator as well. She also knew how to guilt Rene into doing what she wanted.

"I hear ya, Mama. I'll be sure to get them over there to see you this weekend," Rene assured her.

"Okay, baby. Sounds good. Call me after your test."

"You know I will. Love you."

Hearing those words from her youngest daughter always warmed Ms. Martha's heart. "I love you too."

Throughout her entire life, Rene had had her mother to depend on. Not to rescue her from trouble or prevent her from doing things on her own, but she was more like a lifeline. She was steady support to help her get through tough times.

As Rene sat in her driveway trying to gather her thoughts before she went inside to start on her wifely and motherly duties, she let out a deep sigh and smiled. Her long journey of juggling school, home, and a dead-end job would all be over soon. The struggle of living check to check and so many sleepless nights had turned Rene into a determined, hard-core, mentally tough woman. She felt like she could conquer the world if she had to.

"Hey, everybody! I'm home!" Rene bellowed as she entered her three-bedroom townhouse. She dropped her book bag and walked into the den.

"Mommy!" two little voices screamed out as she entered the room. The smiles on her children's faces made her feel invincible.

"Hey, babe," her husband, Jalen, said as he planted a nice, wet kiss on her lips. "You look tired. I guess reading all those books and studying is starting to kick your butt, huh?"

"Like you would never believe!" answered Rene. "I will be glad when all this is over."

"Me too. Then you can start bringing home the bacon, and I can go on vacation," joked Jalen.

They both laughed and hugged as they continued to enjoy each other.

"Damn! Don't you two have a room for that?" said a scratchy voice sarcastically.

Rene turned to see her best friend, Nina, coming down the stairs with her 5-month-old son, Jacob.

"Don't be jealous." Rene smirked.

Nina frowned and scrunched up her face. "Oh, please! Jealous of what?"

"What the fuck does that mean? What you trying to say, Nina?" asked Jalen, moving his arms from around Rene's waist and moving toward Nina.

"How was your day, girl?" said Nina as she threw her hand up at Jalen and changed the subject.

"Long!" answered Rene as she plopped down on the sofa. "I feel like my brain is going to explode."

"Well, nobody told you to work full-time and go to school full-time all while having a family," Nina reminded Rene.

"I know, girl, but what would I do without you?" Rene said as she smiled at her friend.

"Probably die from exhaustion."

When Nina was seven months pregnant with Jacob, she and her then-boyfriend Tyrese had a huge fight. He threw all of her things over the balcony of the luxury apartment they shared, and he refused to have anything to do with Nina or the baby. Nina never really would go into detail of how the fight started or even what it was about. She didn't have a job or an education. All of her family either lived in another state, were opportunists, or were strung out on drugs and alcohol. She had nowhere to go. Her only refuge was with her best friend.

This pattern of chaos was pretty much how their relationship had been since day one. When the two girls met in middle school, it was very clear that they came from two different worlds. That never stopped them from being friends and eventually becoming inseparable.

Although Rene's parents were divorced, they both were essential in her upbringing. They always worked as a team to make sure Rene, her older sister, and her two younger brothers were handling their business inside and outside of school. Her parents were old-fashioned and strict. Rene was involved in school, played sports, and interned every summer. Everyone loved her, and her future was important to her.

Nina's life was the exact extreme opposite. Her mother worked two jobs to try to support herself and her three girls. However, the fast street and party life was just as important to her. Nina's mother, Nichelle, was often either not at home or at home entertaining guests at her infamous basement parties. Nichelle also was a huge fan of the bars' male population, and she had several one-night stands and short-term boyfriends in and out of their home.

Nina's father stayed plagued with trouble Nina's entire life. He was constantly in and out of prison for crimes like robbery and drug possession, all of which were a direct result of his addiction to alcohol and crack cocaine. This hard-core behavior was a way of life up until he was murdered during a dice game when Nina was 14 years old.

Her mother did not handle the death of her father very well and eventually got hooked on drugs and alcohol herself. She quickly went into a downward spiral. They often went with little to no food. Their mother would disappear for days at a time, and she eventually lost her job and had to get on state assistance. Things took an even harder turn toward disaster one month after Nina's fifteenth birthday. From that moment forward, Nina and her sisters' lives became a living nightmare.

Chapter 1

Nina's Story

"Nina. Nina, come here, baby," Nichelle's cracking voice rang out, giving all of her daughters chills.

"Yeah!" Nina yelled down the stairs.

"Don't 'yeah' me, little girl. Come see what I want," Nichelle snapped without raising her voice.

Nina slowly walked down the stairs. She could smell the scent of a man, and the closer she got to the bottom of the stairs, the better she could see the tall, semi-muscular, dark-skinned man, wearing a cognac-colored leather jacket with a dark blue hoodie, blue jeans, and Timberland boots, standing next to her mother in their living room. Her heart dropped to the bottom of her stomach. She could feel that something was not right.

"Yes? What is it, Mama?" Nina asked with fear seeping from her voice.

"Do you remember my friend Bruno?" Nichelle asked her daughter.

"A little bit," answered Nina.

Bruno smiled at Nina. His smile was sweet, but his eyes were dark and evil.

Nichelle's lip began to tremble. She looked at Bruno with despair and desperation, but he did not seem to be moved with a drop of compassion.

"Well, baby, Bruno is going to take you home with him. Just for a few days," Nichelle informed Nina.

Nina became terrified. "But why? Did I do something wrong?"

Nichelle once again looked at Bruno, this time with tears in her eyes. "Please, Bruno. Don't make me do this," she pleaded.

"Bitch, I'm not trying to hear that shit. Either give me my money or give me something worth my money. Those are your only options," he reiterated as he stared at Nina.

Nichelle gathered her thoughts and continued to try to soothe Nina. "No, baby. You didn't do anything wrong. Mama just needs your help. You wanna help your mama, right?" she asked.

"Yes, I do," Nina said with sadness in her voice and fear in her eyes.

Nichelle grabbed Nina and held her close. Tears were streaming down her cheeks. She knew that what she was about to do was one of the most despicable and unforgivable things she could have done as a mother. However, the addiction that haunted her spirit always seemed to be bigger and stronger than her love for her children or for herself.

"Just take me, Bruno," Nichelle said as she stepped in front of Nina and once again began to plead. "I'll do whatever you want. Just please—"

"Bitch, please. Do you really think I want yo' used-up dope fiend ass? Half the niggas in the hood done had they dick in one of your nasty-ass holes! I can do a lot more with this sweet, tender piece right here," Bruno responded as he reached out and grabbed Nina's hand.

Nichelle hung her head in embarrassment when Bruno spoke in front of her daughter about all the men she had been with. Although it was true, it wasn't something she was proud of, and it definitely wasn't something she would have ever shared with her children.

"Come on, Bruno. Don't do this! She's only fifteen," pleaded Nichelle.

Bruno smirked. "Fifteen, huh? Perfect! That's just how I like 'em: young, ripe, and pure."

"Mama, please! Please don't make me go. Please!" Nina begged her mother while squeezing her hand.

Nichelle slowly pried her daughter's fingers loose from hers. "It's okay. You'll be back home soon. I promise."

Nina's sisters, who were only 13 and 10 at the time, sat at the top of the stairs holding and consoling each other, terrified as to what was going to happen to their sister. The cries and pleads for help that flowed from Nina made them cringe and hold each other even tighter.

Bruno snatched Nina to him and walked toward the door.

"Let me go!" yelled Nina. She hit Bruno in his arm, hoping it would force him to loosen his grip. Bruno snatched Nina up by both of her arms and held her so close to his face she could smell the Juicy Fruit gum he was chewing.

"Listen and listen good, little girl," Bruno snapped, talking through his teeth. "This can be as painless or as painful as you make it. You take care of Bruno, and Bruno won't beat the shit out of you. You dig?"

Nina's eyes were big and wide, as though she had seen a ghost. The dark look in Bruno's eyes, accompanied by the pain running down her arms from his grip, let her know that he meant exactly what he said.

She nodded in agreement, then lowered her face and let her tears fall to the floor.

As the two pulled up to Bruno's building, she was shocked and a little relieved. She thought they were going to one of the run-down trap houses in her Detroit neighborhood, or maybe the low-income high-rise a few miles away that was known for its high crime and drug activity.

Instead they were in the suburb of Royal Oak, Michigan, pulling up to a gated apartment complex. The grass was a bright green, luxury cars filled the complex, and the glare from a sparkling swimming pool lit up a bike path.

Once inside, Nina sat down on a black leather couch with her hands under her thighs. She looked around the room, stunned at how nice but messy it was. Her body slowly went numb, and her thoughts drifted between wondering what her sisters were doing and trying to figure out why her mother had chosen her to pay her debt. Not that she wanted her sisters to be there either, but why her?

Bruno's deep voice broke Nina's trance. "Your mama owes me a lot of money, and you need to work off her debt. You can start with this kitchen and then the living room. The cleaning shit is under the sink. Mop and broom are in that closet right there. Don't take forever doing that shit either," he ordered.

Nina nodded to show she understood. She quickly went to the kitchen, following Bruno's directions. The kitchen was a total mess. Dirty dishes were scattered along the counters and filled the sink. Takeout containers and bags covered the stove and the overflowing garbage can in the corner. The stench from all of this almost made Nina throw up.

She held her composure and quickly went to work. After she finished washing all the dishes, taking care of the trash, and mopping the kitchen floor, she went into the living room, another room that looked like a disaster area.

Clothes, shoes, jewelry, money, and even a couple of empty condom wrappers were scattered everywhere. The glass and marble table that sat in the middle of the floor was covered with newspapers, club flyers, marijuana ashes, ashtrays, more food containers, and wrappers. A thick layer of dust seemed to cover everything.

As Nina cleaned, she found all types of money. Stacks of it. A total of $786 to be exact. She did not take a dollar. She stacked the money up as she found it, placing it on the counter in the kitchen.

As she was vacuuming, Nina thought maybe if she continued to work hard and show some sense of loyalty to Bruno, he wouldn't hurt her or her mom. Maybe he would have a change of heart.

Nina wrapped the cord around the vacuum and placed it back into the utility closet. Just as she was doing that, Bruno came out of his room and into the living room.

He was shocked at how clean Nina had gotten everything.

"Damn, girl. This muthafucka hasn't looked this good in over a year," Bruno joked.

Nina just stood there, stiff and emotionless.

Out of the corner of his eye, Bruno spotted the money on the counter. "What the hell is this?" he asked as he picked up the pile of bills.

"I found it," Nina managed to mumble.

"Found?" Bruno asked as he walked toward Nina. "Found where?" He reached out and grabbed Nina's face, squeezing her cheeks tight enough for her to feel the discomfort but loose enough for her to still talk.

"In your stuff! All the stuff in the living room and on the floor!" Nina bellowed as quickly as she could.

Bruno loosened his grip and started counting the money. The odd amount let him know two things. One, the cash was what was left of his drunken nights at the bars and strip clubs, the nights he stripped and passed out on the couch. The second thing it told him was that Nina was not a thief. Whether it was because of fear or because she just wasn't that type of person, her not taking one dollar left a good impression with Bruno.

"Is this all the money? Did you steal from me, bitch?" he yelled.

"No! I promise I didn't take anything!" Nina shared, trying to be as convincing as possible. "Every dollar I found is right there."

"What else did you find? Tell me!" Bruno shouted.

"Nothing!" Nina cried out. "I just found the money. I promise!" She began to sob.

Bruno gave one of his devilish smirks and let her face go. "Smart girl." He walked away and sat on the couch. He turned on his forty-two-inch floor-model big-screen TV and started watching a movie.

Nina continued to stand, not moving a muscle. She wasn't sure what to do. Bruno saw her standing and quickly became agitated.

"Damn, girl! What the fuck is wrong with you? Sit yo' ass down! You making me nervous!" Bruno snapped.

His sudden loud demand startled Nina. She jumped and then quickly walked over to the recliner on the other side of the room and sat down.

"What's your name again?" Bruno asked.

"N . . . Nina. It's Nina."

"Nina. Right. I'ma call you NiNi. I like that better. You look like a NiNi. Stand up and turn around slowly," Bruno instructed Nina.

Nina slowly stood up. She was so uncomfortable and afraid. Her heart was racing, and her palms were sweating. She slowly turned in a small circle. Once she was again facing Bruno, she noticed that he was rubbing his penis. Her heart sank to the bottom of her stomach.

"Go take a shower and clean yourself up. Towels are on the shelf in the bathroom," he ordered.

Nina was hesitant to get up, but she knew that if she didn't, there would be hell to pay, or worse.

As she entered the bathroom and started to close the door, Bruno yelled out, "Nah. Leave that open."

Nina honored his request.

As the warm water hit her body, she couldn't help but find it refreshing. The shower at her house was never as warm, and the water pressure was not as strong. She almost forgot where she was until Bruno came into the bathroom.

"Hey!" he called out from the doorway.

Again startled, Nina jumped. "Yes?"

"There's some shorts and a T-shirt here on the counter for you to put on when you get done. Are you hungry? You eat pizza?" asked Bruno.

Nina was thrown off. Why was he being so nice? "Yes. I like pizza."

"A'ight. I'll order some. When you're done, go into the bedroom."

As he slowly walked away, he caught himself staring at Nina's silhouette through the frosted shower curtain. She was young, but her body was amazing in his eyes.

When Nina was finished, she dried off and slipped into the shirt and shorts Bruno left for her. As she walked into his bedroom, she came to the realization that he probably was going to rape her or make her do sexual things.

Nina was technically still a virgin. She had never had sex, but she had fooled around with a couple of boys before, mostly rubbing and kissing. She never liked anyone enough to go any further. Tonight, she knew she more than likely was not going to have a choice in the matter.

Nina sat on the bed quietly. She was so nervous her stomach was doing flips, and she was biting down pretty hard on her bottom lip. A loud buzz rang out in the apartment.

"Yeah?" Bruno yelled into the intercom.

"Domino's!" the voice on the other side responded.

Bruno hit the button and let him in.

About five minutes later, Bruno entered the room with a box of pizza, some wings, two cans of pop, and some napkins. He placed everything on the bed.

"Go ahead and eat," he instructed Nina. "Dem wings are mine. You can eat as much of that pizza as you want."

Nina's hunger must have been stronger than her nervousness, because without hesitation she flipped the pizza box top open, grabbed a slice, and took a big bite, burning the roof of her mouth.

"Shit! It's hot!" she mumbled with the bite of pizza still in her mouth.

Bruno cracked a smile and shook his head.

He took off all of his jewelry and laid it on the dresser. He then took off his shirt and jeans and hung them on the closet door before climbing into bed with just his wife-beater T-shirt and boxers on. He motioned for Nina to scoot over, and she did so quickly.

"Have you ever seen Friday*?" Bruno asked. "The movie with Ice Cube and Chris Tucker?"*

Nina shook her head. "No. I want to though."

"Cool. I just got the DVD. We can watch it." Bruno grabbed a small remote on his nightstand and pushed play.

As the two ate and laughed at the movie, the curiosity in Nina began to get the best of her. Why was Bruno act-

ing like they were the best of friends? He was so mean at the house. She just didn't get it. Without realizing it, she found herself staring at him.

Bruno caught her stares out of the corner of his eye. He paused the movie. "What the fuck?" he snapped. "Is there a problem?"

"No. No problem. But . . . but . . ." Nina tried to respond.

"What? Spit that shit out!" Bruno ordered.

Nina was able to get the lump in her throat to go away. "Why are you acting like this?"

Bruno looked confused. "Like what?"

"Nice," Nina answered. "Are you going to kill me?"

Nina's blunt words caught Bruno off guard.

"Nah, li'l mama. I'm not gon' kill you," he said while laughing. "Relax and stop staring at me. That shit is weird as fuck."

"But you were so mean earlier. How do I know you're not lying?" Nina asked with tons of doubt still lingering in her voice.

"You don't," he answered. "I'll be one hundred wit' you. What I had planned on doing was working the shit out of yo' li'l ass, making you do some runs in the hood and putting yo' ass on the stage at my club."

Nina's eyes got big like a deer in headlights. "The stage? As in stripping?" she asked.

Bruno nodded. "But in the small amount of time we've spent together, you made me change my mind. You different. You not like ya stupid-ass mama. That might hurt your feelings, but it's the truth. Accept it now so it won't hurt you later. I know. My mama was a dumb-ass dope fiend too."

"Was? What do you mean she was?" Nina asked in a soft and sad voice.

"She's dead. Drug overdose. I never shed one tear for her. Just like she never shed a tear for me," Bruno coldly explained.

Nina dropped her head as tears began to roll down her cheeks. It did hurt to hear that about her mother. She wasn't always this way. However, this was life's reality, and Bruno was right. Nina needed to stop making excuses for her mom.

Bruno grabbed Nina's chin and turned her face toward him. "Wipe ya face. Suck that shit up." He handed her a napkin. "If you listen, if you trust me, and if you stay loyal, I promise you I will not only always look out for you, but I'll teach you everything you need to know about these streets, the hustle, and how to get money. You take care of Bruno, and Bruno will take care of you." Bruno grabbed Nina's hand and pulled her toward him.

Nina's stomach dropped down to the bottom of her feet. The way he pulled her close and wrapped his arm around her was different. It gave her goosebumps but made her want to melt into the bed at the same time.

"What all do I have to do?" she asked.

"Pretty much what you did today. Come over a few days each week, clean up, get my money together for me, stuff like that," Bruno explained. "And give me some of that pretty ass of yours when I want it. I'll make sure you have money in ya pockets. I'll make sure nobody fucks with you or your sisters."

"Whoa!" Nina said as she put both of her hands on Bruno's chest. "I'm not a ho!"

"Girl, hush! Kill that kid shit you talking," hissed Bruno. "I didn't say you had to fuck the whole team. I said me. And only me. You'll be mine and mine alone. I want yo' ass. But I ain't no fucking rapist. This is gonna be an agreement between us."

She wasn't sure if how she was feeling was the right thing to be feeling. She suddenly wasn't afraid, but flattered. Bruno was the man in her world. A big deal!

"You want me? Really? But you're grown."

"I'm not that much older than you. I just turned twenty last month. I've been in these fucking streets for a while, so everybody thinks I'm older than I am. You a virgin?" Bruno asked, not letting up at all.

Nina hesitated but eventually answered his question. "Yes, I'm a virgin."

Bruno smiled. "I knew I was right about you. Don't worry, NiNi. I'll make this night a moment in your life you'll never forget."

Bruno leaned forward and kissed Nina while gripping the back of her neck. As he moved his tongue around in her mouth, Nina didn't fight back or push him away. She allowed her tongue to relax and tango with his.

As if she were a puppet, Bruno pulled her head back and kissed and licked her neck. His kisses were soft yet aggressive, and Nina liked it.

He got on his knees, sat Nina up, and pulled the T-shirt she was wearing over her head. Her perky C-cup breasts stood at attention as she lay back on the bed. She quickly covered them with her arm.

"Nah. Don't do that," Bruno said as he removed her arm. "You're beautiful. A bad bitch! Your body is banging. Be proud of that shit. You don't have a reason to be ashamed or embarrassed. This is about to be my body. Don't ever cover my shit up. You understand?"

"Yes. I understand." Nina looked Bruno dead in his eyes.

Bruno slowly slid Nina's shorts down her legs. They were so big on her it wasn't a very difficult thing to do. As she lay there completely naked, Bruno allowed his eyes to roam her body, admiring every curve, every freckle, every inch of her body. His manhood admired her as well and bulged out of his boxers. He grabbed Nina's hand and placed it on the hard pole.

"Wow!" Nina whispered. She had touched a penis before, but never one this big, never one this long, and never one so hard and throbbing.

"You like that big dick?" Bruno asked.

"I don't know. It's kind of scary," Nina answered honestly.

Nina's blunt yet innocent response made Bruno want to make Nina his even more. "You'll like it soon enough. Trust me."

Bruno gently lay on top of Nina and picked up where he left off. He continued to kiss her neck and slowly made his way down to her breasts. As he massaged one of her breasts, he took the other in his mouth, gently sucking on her nipple, using the tip of his tongue to trace it.

Nina let out a soft moan despite trying her hardest to hold it in. Bruno was nothing like the boys she had dealt with. He got pleasure from pleasing her. Nina didn't think that was possible. Her mother always talked about what she needed to do to make a man happy or make a man want to be with her. She never talked to Nina about getting the things that made her feel good. The more he kissed, licked, and rubbed her, the more her stiff body relaxed and accepted the sensations that were slowly taking over her body.

Bruno could feel Nina getting more and more relaxed, something that he needed to make sure happened. Nina allowing her mind to be free and take pleasure in what he was doing signified trust in him. Trust and loyalty were everything in his world. They were nonnegotiable from those in his circle, especially from any woman he was dealing with.

Bruno inhaled Nina's scent as he made his way down the rest of her body. Her smell was intoxicating, so fresh and sweet. Once he kissed her past her belly button, Nina grabbed his face with both of her hands, signaling for him to stop.

"What? Why you stopping me?" Bruno asked with confusion and a little frustration.

"What are you doing?" Nina asked. "You can't kiss down there."

Bruno shook his head. "You've got to be fucking kidding me," he mumbled to himself. "Just relax. Stop talking. Let me do what I do."

Nina closed her eyes really tight to embrace what was about to happen to her. When his tongue touched her clit, her eyes jolted open and her back slowly grew into a perfect arch off of the bed.

Bruno licked circles around her love box, being sure to not leave one spot out. Nina's moans got louder and louder. Her back was now completely elevated off the bed, with her head thrown all the way back, barely touching the pillow.

"Oh, my God! Please stop! Something is happening! Bruno, please!" Nina pleaded with pleasure.

Nina's cries for mercy only fueled Bruno's desire to continue to please her. He dug his face in deeper, gripping her thighs and paying special attention to her swollen and throbbing clit.

Nina yelled out with pleasure as her legs began to shake and tears rolled down the side of her face. The warm sensation that had begun to grow in her belly had exploded and was now taking over her entire body. She was so numb yet super sensitive to any touch.

"What did you do to me?" Nina huffed as she tried to catch her breath.

"I made you cum," confirmed Bruno. "Did you like it?"

"Yes! A lot!" Nina answered quickly. "I feel funny though. Is my heart supposed to be beating this fast?"

Bruno chuckled. "Yes, NiNi. That's normal. Now go to sleep."

Nina was shocked. Going to sleep was not something she saw in her near future, but she did as she was told.

Bruno went to the bathroom and got a washcloth to clean his face. He then took one in the bedroom and wiped Nina's love box and legs. He got in the bed and went to sleep also.

The next day as Nina rode in the car with Bruno to the mall to buy some clothes and shoes, she couldn't help but have flashbacks of her night and morning. Bruno had finished his Sex 101 lessons with Nina, showing her the proper way to give him head and finally taking her virginity. His penis was so big it took a lot of tries before he could get more than the head in. It hurt so bad in the beginning, but eventually Nina got used to it. Bruno promised her that the more they had sex, the more she would enjoy it and the more he would teach her.

This was the beginning of the four-day stretch that ultimately changed Nina's life and created the monster she would become. It was when she learned that she was no longer a little girl, but a survivor with no room for feelings, remorse, or fear.

After a year of being with and working for Bruno, Nina was a bonified hustler. Her sisters needed her to be. Their mother's addiction had hit an all-time low, and she was a complete prisoner to the drugs.

Nina worked in Bruno's strip club cleaning up the dressing rooms and helping the top strippers collect all their money. She even waitressed sometimes when they were short-staffed. Spending so much time in the club allowed Nina to pick up the skill of boosting. No one taught her directly. She learned all she needed to know by simply eavesdropping on a few of the strippers' conversations.

Nina was a quick learner and smart like that. Before long, working her odd jobs for Bruno, working in the club, and selling the clothes and bags she was stealing, Nina was making anywhere between $1,200 and $1,500 a week. Her sisters totally depended on her, and she was up for the challenge.

Then, just as quickly as Nina's world was on a high note, she took another crucial blow that turned it upside down. Bruno was indicted on drug charges and was denied bail. During that time, the club was shut down, and Nina had no clue where Bruno kept his real money. She had no way to get cash.

To make matters worse, Nina's mother found a new dealer to buy her poison from. His name was Jig.

Jig was a little older than Bruno. His name rang bells and set fear in people's hearts. He was known for three things: being a cold-hearted killer, not taking no for an answer, and beating on women.

Like déjà vu, the day came when Nichelle once again could not pay off her debt and offered up her daughter as a substitution. Nina knew the chances of Jig treating her like Bruno had were slim to none. She had heard tons of horror stories about Jig and how he treated women. He would not care that she was only a teenager. He would rape her and pass her around like it was nothing.

Exactly six months after Nina's sixteenth birthday, she decided her life would be so much better if she'd just raised herself. No more worrying about strange men coming into her or her sisters' bedrooms. No more hiding her valuables and money so that her mother wouldn't sell them. It would all be over.

Nina called her grandparents, who lived on the other side of the city, and begged them to take in her sisters. They were the only family the girls had in the area. Her grandfather at first said no. The couple was on a fixed income and could not afford to have the girls there.

Nina was devastated but did not give up. She finally was able to convince her grandmother to agree. As long as Nina gave them money every week to assist with the girls' care, their grandparents said they could stay until they finished high school.

Nina knew it would be tough, but she didn't care. It had to be done. One Sunday morning, with all of their belongings, the three girls took a bus to their grandparents' house. She got them settled in and went on her way. She never told her mother that they were leaving or where they would be staying. Nina did not want her mother harassing her grandparents, so it had to be that way.

Nina moved in with a couple of the strippers she had become friends with at Bruno's club. It wasn't the best situation, but at least Nina felt safe.

Nina's life was chaotic to say the least. Her only refuge and sense of relief was Rene's house. There she could be a kid and do things that normal teenagers do. Rene's mom took the time to teach Nina basic life skills, like how to sew on a button, the proper way to do laundry, how to budget money, and how to cook. She also received the love and affection that every child longs for.

Rene's parents never were too happy about their friendship from its inception. They had a hunch that Nina was exposing Rene to things that they wouldn't approve of. It was obvious that Nina was far more mature than Rene and well versed in the streets.

Their willingness to help a child in need, especially someone who meant so much to their own child, kept them from trying to keep the two apart. Once the two grew up and became adults, their lives continued to go down different roads, but their friendship remained the same.

As they grew into womanhood, Nina had a "party now, pay for it later" attitude. She dated and slept with random guys, usually as a way of manipulating them or using them to get something she wanted. She never held a job for longer than six months, but somehow, she always managed to keep money in her pocket and get all of her bills paid. She did not mind experimenting with different things either. She had gone from working in the strip club to becoming an actual stripper. She worked at several clubs and became well-known in the bar world. Nina got so good at it she became a main attraction, getting paid to travel and dance at clubs all over the state.

In addition to the stripping, short of being a prostitute, Nina had tried it all and then some. She wasn't ashamed of it and didn't care who knew, but she wanted more. Since the death of her father, stability was not something that Nina had experienced in any aspect of her life. It was something that she never imagined would happen and stopped looking for it. That changed with Rene. Stability was something she'd always admired about Rene's life, and she was so thankful that their friendship was the gateway to stability for her.

Rene was a struggling working wife and mother, pushing her way through school to get her degrees in business and marketing. The plans that her parents mapped out for her weren't quite the path she followed. In her sophomore year of college, Rene had married her high school sweetheart, Jalen.

Jalen was the type of guy every parent wanted their daughter to marry. He was hardworking, charming, a great provider, and he treated Rene like a queen. He wasn't too bad looking either. Standing at an eye-catching six feet three inches, with caramel skin, Jalen was definitely easy to look at. He was in great shape with a great body from all his years of playing high school and college football. He had light brown eyes and the biggest smile Nina and Rene had ever seen. Jalen was the guy everybody liked and wanted to be around because of his charming personality and welcoming energy.

Jalen also came from a solid and strong family. His dad was a police officer, and his mom was a 911 dispatcher. He had two older brothers who were in the military and successful in their careers. His parents celebrated twenty-five years of marriage, and Jalen always had both of his parents in the house with him.

Jalen proposed to Rene during one of his football games. He got his coach to get the stadium announcer to pretend that Rene had won a contest, causing her to go to the fifty-yard line at halftime. Once she was there, Jalen came through the cheerleaders standing behind Rene and got down on one knee. The stadium erupted with sounds of joy and admiration. Rene managed to get out a yes in the midst of her tears. They were the perfect couple everyone loved.

Though Rene and Jalen were young, their parents approved of their marriage. They had a small, private ceremony but a huge reception. All of their old high school friends and college teammates were there. Nina was Rene's maid of honor. She also was the mistress of ceremonies at the reception. She got a few of her friends to put on a show for Jalen and Rene. Needless to say, the couple's conservative parents were not pleased! Ms. Martha literally grabbed them all by the arms and dragged them out of the building. Nina didn't understand what the problem was. It was all in love and fun.

That was what Rene loved about Nina. Even when she was out of place, she was always authentic and true to herself.

Soon after their nuptials, Rene became pregnant with their son, Jalen Jr. Two years later, their daughter, Roslyn, was born. Being pregnant and not being able to go to school full-time delayed Rene's graduation. She never gave up. She was determined to do what she always dreamed of, and Jalen supported her 110 percent.

Nina vowed to never settle down. That was, until the day she met her son's father, Tyrese.

As Nina tried to wean herself off the fast life of the stripping world, she started doing temporary job placement. On one assignment, she was sent to work for a private accounting firm. Nina walked into the small but upscale office a little nervous. This was far classier than any place she had ever been employed, and it was somewhat intimidating. She really wanted to make a good impression.

"Hello," Nina called out as she stood in the lobby.

"I'll be right with you," a deep voice answered.

In a few minutes, the most handsome, clean-cut, and breathtaking man Nina had seen in her life turned the corner and was now standing in front of her.

"Wow!" the two said at the same time, captivated by each other.

"I'm Nina, your temp," she barely got out without stuttering.

Tyrese cracked a smile. "Nina. What a lovely name. I'm Tyrese Smalls. This is my firm. Glad to have you on the team."

After Bruno, Nina was never intimidated or afraid of any man except Jig. She had mastered the skills of reading guys and knowing exactly what to do to get them wrapped around her finger and making them her puppet. Now for the first time in a long time, a man had her speechless.

After a few months, Tyrese and Nina grew closer, and their work flirting soon grew into a full-blown romance. Nina was in love, and no matter what she did, she could not shake or fight the feeling. Tyrese fell hard as well. He spent his days and nights wining and dining Nina, showing her that he wanted nothing more than to spoil her and give her everything he felt she deserved.

When Nina found out she was pregnant, the two were beyond excited and could not wait to welcome their blessing into the world.

Although Jalen owned his own successful landscaping business, between daycare, tuition, and monthly bills, the Martins were barely making ends meet and were in jeopardy of losing their home. The stress of life was also starting to take a toll on their marriage.

Jalen was hardly ever home, and when he was, helping around the house was not something he seemed eager to do. Rene was so consumed with caring for their kids, maintaining the household, and studying, Jalen often was left off of her daily to-do list.

During this same time, Nina came home one day to find Tyrese in a full-blown rage putting all of her belongings out of the house. He had packed up most of her things and set them outside in the front yard. Some items were in bags, and others were scattered around the lawn and sidewalk.

"Tyrese! What the fuck?" Nina cried out as she jumped out of her car and started running toward the front door.

"Get out of my house, bitch!" he snapped back. "I'm done with yo' triflin' ass!"

Nina was stunned. She had no idea why Tyrese was behaving this way. That morning when she left, every-

thing was fine, and now Tyrese was acting like a crazy man and breaking up with her.

"Can you please just calm down? Talk to me! I don't understand what is happening!" Nina pleaded as she scrambled to gather her items off the grass.

"Fuck you!" Tyrese responded. "We don't have shit to talk about. I don't know why I thought your gutter-rat ass could change. Once a hood rat, always a hood rat. Hurry up and get the fuck off of my property! And you're fired, ho! Don't come to my place of business ever again." Tyrese grabbed a black garbage bag full of Nina's shoes and tossed it out the door.

Nina fell to her knees and started sobbing. "What did I do? Please! Don't do this. What about our baby? Our family?" she continued to plead while rubbing her big belly. "I'm about to deliver your son! You do this to me now? Where am I supposed to go?"

Tyrese covered his face with his hands to hide the tears that were now streaming. To hear her say "your son" burned a hole in his heart that felt like it would never heal. He had to push through the pain and stick to his plan.

"What baby? That's not my kid. Leave me alone, and don't ever contact me again! You did this to us! Now deal with the consequences," said Tyrese as he threw one last bag into the yard and quickly slammed the door.

"Tyyyrreesseee!" Nina screamed as she cried, still kneeling in the grass.

Nina was devastated and heartbroken. Tyrese gave her the life she'd always dreamed of and the perfect baby boy to go along with it. They had made so many plans for their future, and just like that, it was over, and Nina had no clue why. The breakup was not only devastating, but it left Nina helpless and homeless with a brand-new baby.

To help Rene and Jalen save some money, Nina moved in with them. In return, Nina would take care of the kids, get them ready for school, drop them off and pick them up, feed them, and anything else that needed to be done. She became, you could say, their nanny.

At first, Jalen was a little reluctant to agree to this. Nina was a little on the wild side, and he wasn't sure if she was responsible enough to care for his children. Rene assured him that everything would be okay. She knew that, outside of them, nobody loved their kids as much as Nina did, and she would always make sure they were okay. After a night of conversing and convincing, Nina moved in.

As soon as Rene's other friends and sisters got wind of this, they raised hell with worry and concern. "What are you thinking?" "Why are you letting that trash move in with you?" "She is gonna get you robbed!" were just a few of the comments that Rene received. She ignored it all. No one ever understood her friendship with Nina, and she didn't expect that to change, nor did she care. Although she loved her circle, Rene always did what she felt was best. No one could control her.

Rene was a sexy and classy woman. She stood at a stunning five feet ten inches (without heels) and had a smile that caught the attention of anyone who could see it. Although she had two kids, she had an awesome body, with all the curves and bumps to match. Her golden brown tone and almond-shaped eyes often made it hard to tell what ethnicity she was. Her hair always looked like she had just stepped out of the salon: beautiful, long, full of bounce and life. She had a natural look: little to no makeup, with an earth-tone gloss on her perfectly shaped lips. It accented her elegant appearance perfectly. She was intelligent and made anyone around her feel like they could do anything. She didn't go out much and had devoted her whole life to her husband, her children, and her education. Loyalty was everything to her, and it showed in her marriage and friendships.

Nina, on the other hand, was quite the opposite. Her face was not much to look at, but she'd always had an amazing body. Her sense of style never left the stripper stage. She always wore tight-fitting outfits that left little to the imagination.

Nina was the definition of ghetto-fabulous, from the way she talked to the way she walked. You never knew if she was going to have on a blond bob-cut wig or be rocking a spiked, short red haircut. She would even wear a thirty-inch weave from time to time. Nina felt as if looking fly was something she was just born to do. From her ever-changing hairstyles and eye color, to the multicolor extensions on her nails, to the skintight outfits she wore, she knew she looked good. Nina would be quick to curse you out if you dared say anything different.

Nina's teeth had small gaps between them, and she always found a reason to be loud and annoying to show them off. Unlike Rene, Nina had a hard-core, bad-ass attitude to match her unique appearance. She was always into it with someone and never really cared about what others thought or how they felt. Rene was the only exception to this rule.

Nina was compassionate and relaxed around Rene. She would turn into a different person. Nina simply adored Rene and would do all she could to make sure she had Rene's back, and Rene felt the same way. So, when Nina moved in, the two could have not been happier. Despite what everyone else said, Rene knew Nina loved her. They were more like family than friends, and there wasn't anything that could ever change that.

Chapter 2

The Beginning of It All

Rene had been a working woman for almost nine months, and things at home seemed to finally be in a great place for Rene and Jalen. In the few months she had been at the marketing firm, she was already the top account representative and was up for a managerial position.

Jalen's business was doing better than ever. Thanks to a huge account he'd picked up from one of the biggest building management companies in the area, his landscaping business was operating in the black for the first time ever, and he was no longer out in the field. His crew had almost doubled, which allowed him to stay in the office and manage the business from there. He never had to even pick up a shovel.

With everything going so well in her family, Rene felt it was a good time to get Nina motivated to start being more productive. She'd convinced Nina to start cosmetology school, and she too was doing great. Instead of always hustling and trying to get over on guys, she started braiding hair and making wigs to earn her money. Nina was really good at both and soon had a solid clientele. Rene was so proud of her, and Nina knew it.

After a long day in the office, Rene could not wait to get home. When she walked in the door, the aroma of lasagna quickly filled her nostrils. She let out a sigh of relief. Nina had fixed dinner, and Rene was so grateful. She dropped her briefcase on the floor and slowly walked to the couch and flopped her exhausted body down.

Nina laughed. "I guess it's safe to say you had a rough day?" she asked. She walked to the couch with a glass of ice water and a plate with a nice-sized piece of lasagna on it to hand to Rene.

Rene peeked out of one eye and saw Nina standing there with the gifts of love. She quickly sat up. "Bless ya heart!" She thanked Rene as she grabbed the food and drink. "I am starving!"

"I could tell. You look dry," Nina joked.

Rene gave Nina the middle finger and then shoved a forkful of lasagna into her mouth. "Where are the kids?" inquired Rene.

"Upstairs," Nina answered. "Everyone is bathed and ready for bed. All homework is completed. Everyone's school clothes are ironed and laid out for the morning."

"You are the bomb!" praised Rene as she inhaled another forkful of food.

"Oh, I know."

Rene just laughed and shook her head. Nina always made her laugh. "Are you still going to feel like doing my hair tonight?" asked Rene. "I'm sick of my head. I really need something convenient."

"Yeah, yeah. I got you," Nina responded.

After she finished her dinner, Rene jumped in the shower and washed and blow-dried her hair. Having Nina in the house helped Rene out so much. Even though Nina did not pay any bills, Rene felt like she was the one winning. Nina did an awesome job looking after the kids and always did what she could to help make Rene's life just a little bit easier.

"What do you say about us going on a date Friday?" Nina asked Rene as she was braiding her hair.

"Girl, that sounds good to me," answered Rene. "I need a night out. These accounts and needy-ass clients at work have been stressing me out! I find myself doing ten to twelve hours' worth of work in an eight-hour workday. It's wearing me down."

"This is what you wanted, so make it happen, captain! You can handle it," Nina said in a sarcastic tone.

"I know. I know. I'm gonna always make it work. That night out sounds great though," sighed Rene. "Where you wanna go?"

"How about the new sports bar on Livernois? I hear they have some bomb wings, an off-the-chain DJ, and their drink prices are really cheap," Nina replied. "You know I'm ballin' on a budget."

"Okay, cool," agreed Rene. "Let me check with Jalen to see if he has plans. I may need to get a babysitter for the kids."

"A babysitter?" questioned Nina, obviously annoyed. "What the hell? I mean damn! He's so busy he can't even keep his own kids? That's the least he can do considering all that you do around here. You already are bringing in more money. What else do you have to do?"

"Well . . ." Rene hesitated. "You know business has picked up for him, and he has to stay in the office late doing paperwork. He is doing the best he can. Give him a break."

"A break? Girl, bye! He's a husband and father. He's doing the shit he's supposed to do! He always has some lame-ass excuse as to why he can't help more. Working late. I'll bet his ass is working late," Nina mumbled.

Rene sat up and turned to look at Nina. "What is that supposed to mean?" she asked. "Why did you say that?"

"Nothing. Just forget it." Nina shook her head in frustration.

Rene snatched the comb from Nina's hand so that she could no longer work on Rene's hair. "Don't 'nothing' me. Tell me. Why did you say that?" inquired Rene.

Nina once again rolled her eyes and then smacked her lips. "I'm just saying I have dated a lot more men than you have. One thing they all have in common is, at some point in time, they are full of shit. I'm not talking about little shit either. I'm talking about epic, life-changing shit."

Rene squinted in confusion. "Come on, Nina. Not Jay. He's a good guy. Always has been. He's never been the jerk type to keep a lot of secrets or do dumb shit. He's a family guy."

"Girl, wake up!" Nina replied. "Don't be naive. Tyrese was a so-called good guy too. Didn't stop his ass from putting me out on the curb for no fucking reason, did it? With a big-ass belly, pregnant with his seed. Didn't stop him from not giving me so much as a prayer to help take of his kid, did it? Even good guys do dumb shit. They can't help it."

There was an awkward pause and then dead silence. Nina could see that Rene was starting to wonder. It was not Nina's intention to overwhelm her. However, she definitely wanted her friend to be a realist. Jalen seemed like a good guy on the surface, but from Nina's experience, nothing was ever what it seemed. Not with the guys she dated anyway.

"Well, when you ask Jalen if he can 'watch his kids,' make sure you ask if it's okay for Jacob to stay too," Nina said as she tried to change the subject.

"Yeah, okay. No problem," Rene responded.

"If he says he is busy, then what? House party? Wine and tacos?" Nina said jokingly.

Rene laughed. "Wine and tacos? You mean tequila and tacos?"

"Whatever you boogie chicks do. I'm a Henny and wings type of chick."

"If you say so, crazy," Rene agreed sarcastically. "Either way sounds good to me."

"That's what's up! I can't wait. Did you want me to put these braids in a bun, or are you wearing them down?" Nina asked.

"Go ahead and leave them down. Jalen likes them like that."

"Lord! Do you do anything for yourself anymore?" Nina snapped.

"Cut it out! There's nothing wrong with wanting to put a smile on your man's face. You'd know that if you had one," Rene slipped in before she took a sip of her drink.

Nina burst into laughter. "Oh, oh, oh, oh! You got jokes, huh? That was a good one."

The two friends continued to laugh as Nina finished up Rene's hair.

Nina's comment stuck with Rene like Gorilla Glue for the rest of the evening. For whatever reason, she couldn't seem to shake it off no matter how hard she tried. She trusted Jalen without a doubt. He'd never given her a reason not to. Whenever she called him, he answered his phone. She had the pass code to his cell and voicemail. He never hesitated to let Rene know where he was or when he was going somewhere. Even when it was a night out with the fellas, Jalen would text Rene whenever he went to a different bar. He seemed to be an open book. However, she started to wonder if maybe there was something she was missing. Was it possible that Jalen could be doing something other than working late? If so, what?

So many thoughts flooded her brain. Why would he be deceitful? What else could he possibly be doing that would cause him to lie to his wife? Then, like a strong sucker punch to the jaw, a light bulb went off in Rene's head. Could he be cheating with another woman? Was there a chance that it wasn't Jalen's job keeping him out late, but another relationship?

"Of course not!" Rene said to herself. "What is wrong with me?"

Rene said her prayers, then cuddled up with her oversized pillows. She needed to get up early in the morning. She had an 8:00 a.m. meeting she needed to prepare for, so her beauty sleep was a necessity. The partners of her firm would be in attendance, and she needed to bring her A game.

At 11:45 p.m. Jalen still had not made it home.

"'Just got paid, it's Friday night,'" Rene sang as she pulled into her driveway, dancing and clapping her hands to the eighties classic as it blared from her radio. "This is my jam!"

Finally, Friday had arrived, and she couldn't wait to hang out to relieve some stress. Her meeting had gone exceptionally well, and she was looking forward to celebrating with her bestie.

As she opened the door and walked in from the garage, she could hear Jalen and Nina talking. As she listened, she realized that their conversation was more like an argument.

"My wife is not you. She is a real woman. A lady and a queen. Not some wild street whore who runs around town looking for a sponsor like your raggedy ass. You better watch yourself, or I'm telling you—" Jalen yelled at Nina.

"Telling me what, you loser?" Nina yelled back. "Oh, I'm a whore now, huh? Really? Is that what you think? You got a lot of nerve saying some shit like that to me!

You really want to go there? Talking to me, is that what you want to do? If your wife is so precious and pure, why don't you act like it, asshole?"

"Trick, are you crazy?" Jalen began to say before Rene interrupted him.

"Jalen! What in the world is going on here? Why are you talking to each other like that?" Rene asked, shocked and confused.

"I can't stand your boy of a husband! That's why. But no worries, ReRe. I can hold my own," Nina replied in a cocky voice.

"Her name is Rene, you hood rat!" Jalen barked at Nina.

The two began to go at it again. They were yelling so loudly Rene could hardly hear her own thoughts. Her thoughts were all over the map, and she began to grow more and more frustrated.

"Stop it!" screamed Rene. "What is wrong with the two of you? I have enough stress at work. I don't want to have to come home to all of this foolishness and craziness! Whatever it is, suck it up and get over it now! Act like adults and not some ghetto-ass reality TV stars! Thanks for ruining my great day!"

Jalen sucked his teeth and gave Nina a strong "what you wanna do?" look up and down. The grimace on his face would have knocked Nina out cold if looks could carry a punch.

Nina responded by throwing her arms in the air and giving Jalen a look and an old-school fighting stance of her own. "You don't want these problems, dude. G'on 'bout ya business before you get embarrassed in front of your wife," she warned him.

Jalen stuck his middle finger up at Nina as he walked over to Rene. He kissed her on the cheek and whispered in her ear, "Sorry, babe." He patted her on the ass, then walked into the kitchen. He grabbed a beer and headed out to the garage.

Once Jalen was outside and the door was shut, Rene looked at Nina with disgust on her face.

"What? It's not all my fault. Your husband can be a jerk sometimes. But I'm sorry about that, girl," apologized Nina in a soft voice. "I didn't mean to add to your stress level."

"What's the problem? You two have been arguing like crazy lately. I don't like it! What's the deal?" asked Rene.

"It's nothing. You know your husband is a control freak, and I just have to remind him from time to time that we do not share a last name or an X chromosome, so he needs to watch how he talks to me. I'm a grown-ass woman, and my daddy is dead," Nina dramatically stated, trying to get Rene to laugh.

"I guess," Rene replied quietly as she shook her head. "I'm going to try to get a quick nap before we go out." She grabbed her briefcase and headed upstairs.

"Okay. I'll make sure the kids eat. I got you!" Nina assured her.

Rene gave her a thumbs-up as she walked up the stairs without turning around.

Jacob began crying. Nina walked over to his swing and picked him up. As she comforted him, she started to think about her situation. She was supposed to be enjoying life with her son and his father, not living with her best friend along with her dumb-ass husband and children. She loved Rene for looking out for her in her time of need. This just wasn't what she wanted out of life.

After dinner, Jalen got their children ready for bed, while Nina did the same with Jacob.

Nina was as ghetto as they came, but she was a really good mother. When she found out that she was pregnant, she made a vow to give her baby all she had and to never allow him to go through the heartache and pain that she had. So far, she was keeping her promise to herself and to her son. She did a great job with Rene's kids as well. They affectionately called her Aunt NiNi, and if someone didn't know better, they would think that Nina was their blood aunt.

As Rene stood in the mirror applying her makeup, Jalen came into the room. He stood in the doorway admiring his gorgeous wife. The dark ripped jeans she wore hugged the curves of her hips and butt perfectly. The halter top she had on complemented her long neck and perky bustline to a T. He couldn't help but get aroused and wanted to take his wife right then and there.

"Are you sure you just goin' to eat some wings and get drinks?" Jalen asked as he crept up behind Rene, tightly wrapping his arms around her waist and kissing the back of her neck.

Rene smiled and blushed. "Of course, baby," she answered in her seductive voice. She loved the way Jalen was still so attracted to her after all their years together. She always knew she was looking good based on how Jalen responded to her. His strong arms around her still sent a chill up her spine.

Jalen's kisses continued as his hands started to roam Rene's body. Rene closed her eyes and enjoyed her husband's affection. His hands slowly made their way up Rene's shirt, and he began to rub her breasts, softly playing with her nipples. A tingling sensation began to run through Rene's body, making her mouth water and her sweet juices started to flow. Rene began to feel the sensation and desire to have Jalen inside of her.

Jalen knew his wife's body more than she did at times. He knew that playing with her perfectly erect nipples was like pushing the start button on a washing machine. One thing he was certain he had mastered was knowing how to please his wife.

"You look good enough to eat, babe. Let me lay you down and get a little snack before you leave," Jalen whispered in Rene's ear as his hand entered her pants. He could feel the moistness of her love box, and it instantly caused his manhood to throb.

Rene blushed and looked into Jalen's eyes through the mirror. "You can have whatever you want, daddy," she replied to her husband.

Jalen grabbed Rene's underwear and jeans at the same time and slid them down her legs. He turned her around, picked her up, and carried her over to their bed. Before Rene's head hit the bed, Jalen put his face between her legs and rubbed his tongue up and down her throbbing pussy.

Rene squirmed in pleasure as Jalen inserted his index finger and started rubbing the inside of her pussy. Rene moaned with pleasure. Her body was exploding all over. Before she could catch her breath–

Bang, bang, bang!

A knock at the door startled them.

"Girl, hurry up. I'm starving," yelled Nina. "What the hell is taking you so long? You started getting dressed before I did."

"Okay! H . . . here I come! Stop yelling," Rene yelled back, huffing for air. "Babe, I'm sorry, but we're going to have push pause on this session so I can finish getting dressed," Rene instructed Jalen.

"Damn! Come on, bae, don't leave," begged Jalen as he placed Rene's hand on the throbbing bulge in his pants, allowing her to feel the nine-inch rock-hard penis that was leaving an imprint in his sweatpants. "See what you did to me? You really gonna leave your man hanging like this?"

Rene chuckled and kissed Jalen on the lips. As tempting as he was, she had to go. "You did that to yourself.

Now come on. Get up and let me finish getting dressed!" she teased. "You know I've been looking forward to this all week, but I promise you, when I get home, it will definitely be Mommy/Daddy time."

The two embraced for a passionate kiss. Jalen slowly rubbed Rene's thighs. Rene pulled away. "When I get home, Jay!"

"Okay, okay," Jalen said, sulking and walking away.

Rene finished getting dressed and walked out of her room to find Nina sitting on her bed, touching up her newly glued quick weave.

"Are you ready yet?" Nina impatiently asked. "You are taking forever."

"Yes, yes. Come on," beckoned Rene.

"Damn, girl!" Nina said as she checked Rene out in her jeans. "You are wearing the hell out of them jeans! They owe you a check for advertising they shit like that. You gon' be turning heads tonight."

"Thanks! I got these on sale at Nordstrom last week," Rene said proudly. "I was hoping that they fit me right. You know these hips of mine keep me from wearing a lot of cute pants."

"Well, you hit the jackpot with those bad boys. Indeed you did," Nina complimented her.

As the two headed to the door, Jalen yelled to Rene, "Behave, babe! You know I have eyes everywhere. Don't drink too much either. Remember you have a promise to keep when you get back. You have a man, not like your gold-diggin', trash-ass friend."

Rene shook her head. Why Jalen insisted on antagonizing Nina, Rene just did not understand. She blew Jalen a kiss, checked her purse for her wallet and keys, and proceeded to walk out the door.

Nina mouthed, "Fuck you," to Jalen, irritated by his smart-ass comment.

He smirked at Nina and responded, "No, thank you!"

"Man, this boy is off the chain! Hell yeah!" Nina yelled out as they entered the bar. "We should have graced this joint with our presence a long time ago!"

She instantly started swaying her hips to the music playing in the background while Rene looked for a table. The bar was packed and full of mostly young professionals looking to let their hair down. Some neighborhood locals were mixed in the crowd, and they were caught up in the good-vibe atmosphere as well.

There was a game room in the back with a pool table, an old-school Ms. Pac-Man game, and a dartboard. Guys yelled and cheered each other on. Basketball games and Keno played on all the flat screens scattered around the room. The bar was filled with flirting beautiful women trying to catch the attention of the eager men who wanted to impress them and see what was popping for the night.

Rene spotted a high-top table that was available. She grabbed Nina's hand and quickly maneuvered through the crowd to make sure no one beat them to it. Once they sat down, a short, perky waitress came over with menus.

"What are your specials tonight?" asked Rene.

"Tonight we have five-dollar shots of 1800 Silver, Tito's, and Hennessy. Our wings are fifty cents apiece, minimum order of six," answered the waitress.

"Are the wings whole or Wing Dings?" Rene asked.

"Wing Dings. We have four flavors available: plain, lemon-pepper, honey-barbeque, and Buffalo," she proudly responded.

While Rene continued to ponder over the menu, Nina ordered her food. "Let me get a shot of Henny and some Coke on the side with ice. And let me get six lemon-pepper wings fried hard, not burnt!" Nina emphasized.

"No problem! Do you know what you want to order, ma'am?" the waitress asked Rene.

"Ummmm, yes. I will take a shot of 1800 with a splash of cranberry and pineapple juice. Also, I'll take an order of six wings. Half honey-barbeque, half lemon-pepper, and all flats, fried hard please," Rene ordered.

"There you go with that boogie shit," Nina joked.

"Really?" said Rene. "My food order makes me boogie?"

"Did you hear all that shit you just said?" Nina asked while laughing. "Just difficult as hell."

"No, no. You're fine," the perky waitress said to Rene. "It wasn't that bad. I am going to put this order in and get you ladies some water. I'll be back shortly." She picked up their menus and walked toward the kitchen.

"I'll be back. I gotta pee!" Nina informed Rene.

While Rene sat at the table waiting for Nina, the waitress dropped off their water and drinks. Rene started thinking as she sipped.

Although Nina and Jalen didn't always get along, Rene felt like she was the luckiest woman in the world. Nina was such a dynamic friend. Most of the time, Jalen and Nina's arguments would be because Nina felt like Jalen wasn't giving Rene everything she deserved, or because Jalen felt like Rene was too classy a woman to be friends with someone like Nina.

Rene figured it was better to have two people who loved you fighting over your well-being than to not have anyone who loved you at all. However, lately the arguments had been increasing not only in number but also in the level of seriousness. There just seemed to be an awkward and undeniable tension in the air whenever the two of them were in the same room. Nevertheless, Rene loved her life and everyone in it.

Not too long after Nina got back from the bathroom, she spotted her friends Shanequa, Jody, and DJ. She got their attention and waved them over. Rene prayed they would say their hellos and goodbyes quickly and leave. These were the friends of Nina's Rene didn't care for. She was not at all thrilled about them being there.

"Can you fix your face?" requested Nina. "You don't have to look so mean."

"I can't help it. These girls irritate my soul, and I give no fucks if they know it," Rene informed Nina. "Make this conversation quick so they can leave please."

Nina let out a big sigh. Most people thought that Rene was quiet and nonconfrontational and that Nina was her bodyguard, the person who protected her. Nina knew different. Rene could hold her own in a fistfight and had heart that was unmatched. She was not afraid of or intimidated by anyone. She was always nervous that one of her other friends would underestimate Rene, saying or doing something stupid to piss Rene off, and that she would be burdened with the task of pulling Rene off of them. She always prayed silently that all parties would behave whenever they were together.

When the group of ladies got to the table, Rene bit down on her jaw in an attempt to not react to the hot mess standing in front of her.

"Is that my bitch Nina?" said Shanequa as she approached Nina and Rene's table.

"Hey, girl! What's good?" replied Nina.

"Bitch, where you been? What? You don't know us no more? You too good to kick it in the hood?" joked Shanequa, causing the other ladies to laugh, with the exception of Rene.

"Cut it out. You know better than that. I've just been busy," Nina replied.

Shanequa was a simple, low-life stripper, despite the flabby belly and stretch marks that covered it. One would think a gut and unflattering stretch marks would have stopped her from dancing, but it did no such thing. She had six kids by five different guys, and none of her kids lived with her. They all stayed with their fathers or her mother. She had a reputation of doing whatever with whomever for money, and she was proud of it. There was a rumor going around that Shanequa had one of the city councilmen on tape receiving oral sex from her, which was how she was able to drive a big-body Benz, have all the latest bags, and have fine jewelry around her neck and wrists, though she lived in the projects. Since he was married, he gave her whatever she wanted to keep her quiet. Shanequa was as scandalous as they came.

Jody was what Rene liked to call a "shim," she and him combined. Jody made her feel very uncomfortable, partially because she was an open lesbian who took pride in what she called turning straight women out, and partially because of her reputation. She was well-known for being a thief. She did anything from boosting clothes, jewelry, and many other items to taking a credit card straight out of some else's wallet. At first sight, you would think Jody was a guy. She had a low haircut and always had on men's clothing and cologne. The one thing that gave her away was her voice. It was light and almost childlike and didn't fit her masculine appearance. Jody and Nina got close when Jody was a bouncer at one of the strip clubs that Nina used to dance at. She would fight anybody, anytime, anywhere.

DJ was the oddball of the crew. Unlike the other ladies, she was actually rather cute. She was quiet, and you could tell she did not have the rough life that the other two ladies had experienced. DJ was only 19 and would follow the other two women around like a puppy. DJ had been over to the house with Nina before, and Rene thought she was sweet and had the potential to do great things.

DJ was raised by her grandmother, and when she died, she had nowhere to go. Up until her grandmother's death, DJ was a good student and lived a normal life. She never knew her mother or father, but it didn't matter. Her grandmother made sure she never wanted for anything. She gave her lots of love and raised her the right way. After she lost her grandmother, DJ had no money or any other means to take care of herself. Shanequa was DJ's neighbor and took her in. DJ was grateful for Shanequa and felt like she owed her so much. Rene wasn't sure if DJ was a stripper or what, but she didn't seem to belong with that group of ladies.

Whenever Rene questioned Nina about why she even associated with such people, her answer was the same. They helped her get money. She trusted them because of their loyalty to her over the years. Shanequa always had the "hook-up," and Jody had connections with different party promoters and job opportunities.

When Nina danced, Shanequa looked out for her with the other dancers, making sure no one was taking her money or clothes from her locker. Jody always walked her to her car and made sure she was safe and kept the weirdos from harassing her.

Rene constantly encouraged her to find other means to get income. It wasn't that Rene was stuck-up or looked down on them, but in her mind, everything about those two spelled trouble. She did not want them around.

Shanequa cut her eyes in Rene's direction, and her smile quickly left her face. "Well, if it isn't the queen of the bad and boogie crew, Rene. What's up, boo-boo kitty?" she asked, getting a couple of silent laughs from Jody and DJ.

Rene stared Shanequa in her eyes, with a sinister smile on her face. She grabbed her purse and hopped down out of her chair. Nina's heart dropped to the floor. She was anxious, not knowing what Rene might do next.

"Let's be clear, sweetheart," started Rene, getting right in Shanequa's face. "I'd rather be bad and boogie than broke and busted any day! You should use your energy to buy a better weave and a waist trainer. I think doing that would benefit you far more than hating on someone to whom you could never compare."

Rene looked at Nina. "I have to use the restroom. When the waitress returns, please order me another drink, and make it a double. I need some extra help to relax now. I'll be back." She turned and walked away.

Once Rene was far enough away and no longer within hearing distance, Nina gave Shanequa a light push on her shoulder. "Girl! What is wrong with you? I keep telling you, don't let Rene's personality or professionalism fool you. She got hands!" Nina warned.

Shanequa laughed. "I'm not worried about no damn Rene!" she responded with a clear look of shock on her face. "I will dog walk that bitch. Shit, I got hands too, and I'm not scared of her. That skank using them big words or whatever don't do shit but give me headache."

Nina gave Shanequa a cold look. "Watch your mouth. I have warned you about calling Rene out of her name. I don't play that shit! You're no exception to the rule. You don't get a pass," Nina scolded her. "Matter of fact, did you need something? If not, you can walk away now. I'll catch up with you later."

Shanequa knew better than to piss Nina off any more than she already had. She looked over at the other two ladies, and they both were giving her a look that said to let it go.

"Hold on! We came over here to tell you something," said Shanequa, changing her tone and making sure that she was not being argumentative.

"Okay, talk. I'm listening," Nina responded.

"Did you know Bruno is home?" asked Jody.

Nina spit out the water that was in her mouth. "Bruno?" she responded, puzzled. "My Bruno? I thought they gave him thirty years."

"They did," confirmed Jody. "Due to new evidence or some shit like that, he got his case reopened, and they ended up giving him time served. He's been home for about eight months now."

"And he's looking for you," added Shanequa.

Nina felt a big lump in her throat. "For me? What the hell for? I haven't spoken to Bruno in years," she replied.

"He's back in the game," Shanequa began to explain. "He just bought the strip club that got shut down last month on the west side. He needs a manager to handle the girls and the books. Someone he can trust. He said that person is you."

Nina had a blank yet stunned look on her face. "That is crazy. I don't know why he would say that. Besides, it doesn't matter. I'm done with that life."

Shanequa turned her head quickly and looked at Nina. "Bitch, since when?" she asked Nina in a mocking voice.

Nina was not amused. "Don't come for me, ho. After I had Jacob, I told you I had to let that shit go after our last job. I haven't done anything since. I moved on."

"I mean, that's cool. You got ya son now, so I get it, but that money is something that should really make you reconsider coming out of retirement," said Jody. "You already know bitches is lining up to work for Bruno. He gon' have all the celebrities and ballers up in there, and you his right hand. He definitely is gonna make sure you get yours. The pay he offered me to be security is legit. I know your shit gon' be up there."

"Don't be so quick to say no," Shanequa suggested. "At least talk to the man and see what he on. Then make a decision."

Nina's gut was telling her to stay far away from Bruno and anything connected to him. On the other hand, if he was serious about her being his manager, it could give her the extra money she needed to get her and Jacob their own place and finally be 100 percent on her own.

"Fine," Nina began. "Give him my number. Tell him to hit me up so we can talk business."

Jody giggled. "Just business?"

Nina cut her eyes at Jody. "Yes, bitch, just business!"

Jody held her hands up and took a few steps back away from the table. The other ladies laughed.

"All right, girl. You enjoy the rest of your boogie-filled evening," Shanequa said with an attitude as she saw Rene returning. She, Jody, and DJ turned in the opposite direction and walked up to a group of guys sitting at the bar.

"I didn't run your company off, did I?" Rene asked cynically as she sat down.

Nina just shook her head. "Of course you did!"

The two laughed.

"Why do you hate them so much?" Nina asked as the waitress brought their wings.

"I don't hate them. I'm just a strong believer that light and dark can't exist in the same space. One is going to always drive out the other. Those bitches are dark. I'd rather not have them in my presence," explained Rene. She took a bite of one of her wings.

"Now that's not fair. You know tons of people who think and say the same thing about me and you," defended Nina.

"True," Rene agreed. "The difference is it's not true. You are a great person with a huge heart. You just happen to be a product of your environment. When you had a chance to do different, you did."

Rene's words hit Nina a little different. They made her mind start to wonder. She was so grateful that Rene always saw the good in her no matter what was going on in her life at the moment. She also knew that Rene had a lot of confidence in her. If she went back to the strip-club life, she would be taking a huge chance of getting caught up in that lifestyle again and potentially losing her friendship with Rene.

After a few hours passed, Rene and Nina began winding down their night. Nina was right when she said Rene was going to be turning heads. Her gorgeous look motivated one guy to pay for their drinks, and another guy paid for their meal.

"I love hanging with you! We never have to pay for anything!" laughed Nina. "I can keep my little thirty dollars I planned on spending right in my pocket."

"You are a trip!" replied Rene. "I told you not to make eye contact, but you just refuse to listen."

"Ay, we got a free meal and drinks out of it right? Stop all of your fussing, and tell a bitch thank you!" Nina demanded of Rene.

Rene laughed and had to agree with her.

While in the midst of sharing their laugh, Rene glanced up, and a familiar face caught her eye. Her facial expression quickly changed, causing Nina to become concerned.

"Is that . . ." Rene began to say to herself. "No. Couldn't be. I'll be damned, it is! Girl, look! Tyrese's triflin' ass is standing at the end of the bar!" Rene informed Nina while pointing in his direction.

Nina turned around slowly. When her eyes landed on the man Rene was pointing at, her stomach dropped down to her knees. Tyrese was definitely standing there, live and in living color.

After their whirlwind love affair, which lasted a little over two years, Nina never thought she would be without Tyrese. They made plans to one day make their union official and get married. Nina getting pregnant with Jacob made them closer, and for the first time in both of their lives, they were genuinely happy.

In spite of Nina's rough exterior and even rougher attitude, Tyrese was the man who touched her heart and gave her a new outlook on life. He was tall, about six feet five inches, with a milk-chocolate complexion and a goatee connecting to his five o'clock shadow beard. He had a fade haircut that always had a fresh, crisp lineup. He was a successful financial advisor and accountant with deep pockets that enhanced his already undeniable sex appeal.

Once, Nina showed Rene a video of her and Tyrese fooling around, giving each other a strip tease. Rene had to admit to Nina that Tyrese had the biggest penis she had ever seen in her life. He could have made a good living as a porn star. His "third leg" was a whopping thirteen inches when fully erect. Nina bragged that he also had the oral skills of a professional porn star. Their sex life was amazing. Nina had found the perfect guy.

Rene understood fully why Nina was willing to change everything about herself to be with Tyrese. He was a legit and confirmed total package. When Tyrese tossed all of Nina's belongings outside, Rene was shocked. She felt there was no reason big enough to put the mother of his unborn child out in the streets.

"Oh, my goodness. That is him," Nina said as she jumped up out of her chair. "Come on, girl, let's go!"

Nina started to gather her purse. She dropped a $5 bill on the table for a tip, then grabbed Rene's hand. Rene snatched her hand back and frowned at Nina.

"Go? Why the fuck do we need to leave? Forget that deadbeat bastard!" Rene said. "Why do we have to go because he's here? He's the one who should be ashamed and hiding his face. Not you!"

"I just don't want to ruin a good night. Can we please just get out of here? I don't want to make a scene and have everybody in my business. You know this shit can get ugly and quick. It looks like he's with that lady. I don't want any drama. Please, Rene, let's go!" Nina begged her friend.

Rene looked into Nina's face. Something about the look in her eyes almost scared Rene. It was a look of desperation, worry, and fear. It was a look that in the twenty-plus years of knowing Nina she had never seen before. Nina looked as if she saw a zombie walking through the door.

Rene grabbed her purse and stood up out of her chair. "Okay, girl, just calm down. We can go."

The two managed to make it out of the sports bar without being noticed by Tyrese.

During the drive home, Nina was extremely quiet. Two of her favorite songs came on the radio, and Nina did not sing or hum one note of either. It was totally out of her character. At one point, Rene thought she saw a tear rolling down Nina's cheek.

When Rene pulled into her garage, she turned the car off and looked over at Nina. Rene was a little confused. The Nina she knew didn't back down or run away from anyone or anything, and here she'd seen Tyrese, the man who put her out practically with nothing and offered her zero support for their child, and she tucked tail and took off running?

On top of that, Nina being so overprotective of Rene and constantly fighting and fussing with Jalen made her feel that something was wrong. Rene couldn't put her finger on it, but there was definitely something going on in her best friend's life that she wasn't sharing.

"What?" Nina asked Rene when she noticed her looking at her. "Why are you looking at me like that?"

"Girl, are you sure you're okay?" asked Rene. "Your actions tonight were all out of character for you."

"Yeah, girl!" joked Nina. "Don't worry about me. I'm fine."

"Stop it, Nina. Come on now. This is me you're talking to. I know you. Running from a potential fight? Nah. Not your style at all. Then if I throw in all of your fighting with Jalen, none of it adds up. Tell me what's up with you," pleaded Rene.

Nina wanted to share the thoughts running through her head, the things that had her stomach doing flips and the lump in her throat getting bigger and bigger. She just couldn't. She honestly didn't know how or where to even begin.

"ReRe, I'm good. Just leave it alone. Please?" Nina answered.

Rene didn't believe Nina, but she didn't want to push the issue. She figured that when Nina was ready to talk to her about whatever was going on, she would.

The two walked into the house. Nina kicked off the five-inch stilettos she was wearing and went into the kitchen and poured herself a glass of ice water. Rene said good night to Nina and went upstairs.

When Rene opened her bedroom door, Jalen was wide awake, waiting for his wife to return home so he could take her up on the promise she made before she left the house.

Rene was surprised to see that Jalen was still awake. "I thought you would be sleeping by now," Rene said.

"Why would you think that? As good as you were looking and tasting before you left, no way was I falling asleep before I got some of that good stuff!" Jalen replied.

Rene gave him a flirtatious grin. She knew it was time to pay up. She took off her clothes, hanging her jeans in the closet. She then hopped in the shower to get the sweat from chair dancing and the liquor smell off of her. She grabbed her coconut oil and lathered her body with it. Jalen loved when she came to bed with fresh, moist skin, and Rene knew it. Once she was done, she didn't bother putting on any pajamas or even any lingerie. She was fully aware that if she did, they would not be on very long.

As she climbed into bed, Jalen quickly grabbed her by the waist and pulled her to him. He began kissing her face and neck.

"Whoa! Let me get in the bed all the way before you pounce on me!" Rene joked.

"I can't wait any longer," Jalen growled at his wife. "You took too long to get home. That was torture."

Rene decided not to put up a fight, and she gave in to her husband. Not that trying to fight with him would have done any good. He had a way of taking it and making sure that Rene couldn't say no. In his words, "Hers was his and his was hers. No need for permission."

Jalen continued to place kisses all over his Rene. The inside of him was yearning to bring their bodies together and become one. As his kisses were getting lower and lower, Rene's body was melting into the soft cotton sheets on their king-size bed. Jalen knew exactly how and where to touch her to make her body burst with ecstasy.

Jalen grabbed both of Rene's breasts in his hands and nibbled on them until she began to softly moan and rub the back of his head. His kisses then slowly moved down Rene's stomach to her inner thigh. Jalen gently bit her thighs while keeping her breasts in his hands. He then lifted her up slightly and went mouth-first into her pussy, which was already dripping wet with excitement. Feeling her wetness as soon as he touched her caused Jalen's dick to become rock hard.

He began to suck and lick on her clit and pussy walls until her body vibrated with passion and her vagina squirted like a waterfall. Once Jalen was done tasting his wife's goodness, he quickly came up and started to rub his hard, throbbing penis between her breasts. Rene did not mind at all. She loved when he just took control while they were having sex.

As he did this, Rene received her husband's manhood in her mouth, sucking his penis and gently stroking his balls until he became so weak in the knees he had to grab the headboard for support. Once Jalen could not take any more, he flipped Rene over and inserted himself inside of her from behind. Rene arched her back as she received his love. Jalen's strokes became harder and more passionate, going deeper and deeper inside of Rene's warm goodness with every pump.

The depth and gooey wetness that he felt from Rene seemed to get better and better the longer they were together. Before Rene knew it, she was firmly gripping her sheets and biting her pillow as she moaned and softly called out his name. She reached her hand under her stomach and began to rub her clit. She could tell that he was about to climax due to his strokes becoming harder. She wanted to cum on his dick as he was cumming in her. As if they were synchronized, they both let out a long groan as they climaxed together, exploding on each other. Rene came so hard she literally exploded everywhere, squirting and shaking uncontrollably.

"Ohhh myyy God!" Rene yelled out.

"Ohhhh, daddy loves it when you squirt, baby," Jalen expressed. "Tells me that I did a good job making my pussy feel good."

"Yes, you did, daddy," Rene confirmed, trying to catch her breath.

Once they were done, Rene went to the bathroom to get a towel and clean herself up while Jalen got some fresh sheets from the closet and changed the linens on the bed. As she looked at herself in the mirror, she couldn't help but reflect on her life and think about how blessed she was. *How sweet this thing called life is for me! I am one lucky woman.*

She got back in bed and put her head on Jalen's chest. She loved listening to his heartbeat. As her mind and thoughts began to slow down and her climax dwindled away, Rene drifted into a deep sleep.

Chapter 3

Who Knows the Secret?

Ring, ring.

"Hello?" said Nina.

"NiNi! What's going on, beautiful? Did you miss Bruno?"

Nina's heart skipped a beat. She had not heard that voice in so long. She had a different type of affection for Bruno. A part of her resented him for exposing her to the street and stripper lifestyle, forcing her to become an adult way before she needed to. Then on the flip side, she loved Bruno. Because of him, she was able to take care of herself and her sisters while her mother got high and fucked guys for money. Bruno protected her and taught her so much. Thanks to him and all that he had done, Nina would always be able to survive.

"Bruno?" she said. "I don't think I know a Bruno."

"Yeah, okay. You better stop playing with me," he said. "Relax. How you been?"

"Perfect. You know me. I'm gon' always make sure I'm okay. What about you? You married?"

"No, I'm not married. Hell, I'm not in a relationship at all. I did have a baby though."

"Get the fuck outta here! You are somebody's mama? That's incredible."

"Oh, so you got jokes? Yes, I'm somebody's mama. And?"

"Nah, I'm just messing with you. It's good to hear your voice."

"Yours too. Now what do you want?"

"Damn, NiNi, it's like that?"

"Hell yeah, it is."

"Okay. I can respect that. I need you to come help me run my new spot."

"What exactly does that mean? And how much is it paying?"

"I need you to manage the girls. Hire them, watch over them while they are on the clock, and keep them from fighting and arguing all the damn time, you know, the basic shit. I need you to handle the front of the house, too. Make sure the bartenders and waitresses are doing what the fuck they supposed to be doing and not stealing my liquor or my money."

"Sounds like a lot. A lot of work and a lot of bullshit to clean up."

He laughed. "Ay, it is a lot of work and a lot of bullshit. That's why I'm willing to give you a thousand a week plus fifteen percent of the admission fee."

"The door fee? That means you want me to help promote and shit, too. Right?"

"That's why I always fucked with you. You smart as fuck, and you always see the big picture."

"And I see through the game and pimp shit muthfuckas try to run on me."

"I wouldn't do that to you. You know I love you. I wish shit could have started out differently between us, but that was our destiny. It is what it is, and can't either of us change that. Once I really got to know you, I had plans on you becoming my Bonnie. My rida."

Nina lay on her bed, staring at the ceiling, listening to Bruno talk. He was right. Their connection and energy together were undeniable. The circumstances in which they became friends and even intimate with one another was fucked up to say the least. However, Nina would be lying if she said that she didn't feel a sense of loyalty to Bruno, and she loved him. He always knew exactly what to do to make her body go insane. He had the perfect stroke rhythm: not too fast, not slow. Bruno was an amazing kisser. Anytime Rene would embrace in a kiss with him, her pussy would get so wet and she would be so horny. She had to push those memories deep down and not allow them to influence her decision-making.

She said, "Well, that was then. I have to live for right now. I have a little boy to think about now. I'm all he has. Make it twelve hundred a week and you have a deal."

"I understand. I can do twelve hundred. No problem. There's one more item of business I need your help with if you're open to it."

"Damn! You come home with the goal of tryin'a take over the city or something?"

"I don't need to take over the city to make money. I just need my piece of the pot. You feel me?"

"Yeah, I feel you. So, what's this other business you talking about?"

"I got a little gambling spot. An internet café and poker room. That bitch be packed already. It blew up so quick I had to make the poker room invite only."

"Now that's what's up! I used to work at a gambling spot. He had a few internet slot machines, but his main bread came from the poker room. These internet cafés be poppin' and bring in a lot of bank! What would you need my help with?"

"What else? Collect my money! Keep my books."

"Now how in the hell am I supposed to do all this, Bruno?"

"Neither business is open every day. The club is open Thursday through Monday. The café is only open Tuesday, Wednesday, and Thursday. I'm willing to give you anther five hundred a week to run the café, too."

"So, when am I supposed to see my son and take care of my clients? This is too much."

"Come on now, relax. We can figure all that out soon enough. Just tell me that you're on my team again. I'll do whatever I need to make this work for you."

Nina paused before she answered. In addition to making sure she had time for her son, she didn't want to put herself in a crazy position that jeopardized her relationship with Rene. She did not like keeping secrets from her, but this was a lot of money to pass up.

"If you can work around my schedule and give me an even two thousand a week, we can make something happen."

"Damn, NiNi. That's kind of steep."

"That's the only way it would be worth it for me, considering I'm going to miss money doing hair, and my childcare bill is gonna go up. I have to make sure it all makes sense for me."

Bruno let out a deep sigh. "Okay. You got it."

"Cool. Nice doing business with you."

"I got a question. You said earlier that you were all your son had. What the fuck you mean by that? Where's the nigga who knocked you up? He not around?"

"He's around in the city, just not around me or his son. That's a long story that I might share with you one day."

"Meet me for dinner. You can share it then."

"No."

"Wow. Just a flat-out no? Why not?"

"Because I'm not going on a date with you. We are not gonna even cross that line. Everything we do will be a hundred percent business."

"Come on now. It's me. You don't have to be all tough and shit. I just wanna see you. Spend a little time with you. I mean, damn, it's been years since I laid eyes on you. You don't miss the time we spent together? You don't miss how Bruno used to lay that dick down? How wet I used to get that pussy and make that motherfucker throb?"

Nina wanted to say yes to Bruno so badly. She wanted to join him in the sex talk so badly. However, doing that and giving in to him would allow him to regain the power he had over her when she was a teenager. There was no way she could let that happen. She tried to think of something to say and think quickly. Bruno was slick, and once he got on a roll, it would be incredibly hard to resist him.

"It doesn't matter if I miss you. It doesn't matter if I miss your dick. The only thing that matters is us making this money. That being said, I will meet you for lunch, not dinner, and I will be sure to bring my son with me so you can meet him."

Everything about Nina's attitude and responses was turning Bruno on. It had been a long time since he was around a woman he admired and was attracted to the way he was with Nina. Regardless of what she had asked for, he would have given it to her. He just wanted to make sure that he would be around her as much as possible. After all the years that had passed, he still had a weak spot for Nina that didn't seem like it was going anywhere anytime soon.

"Man, you being so difficult! Fine. You have my number now. Text me when you're ready to make it happen. Within the next few days please. I need you on board soon."

"Okay, okay. I'll text you later on today. Goodbye."

Nina's lunch meeting with Bruno, to her surprise, went rather smoothly. They confirmed the $2,000 a week, and for that amount Nina agreed to work at the strip club Thursday night through Saturday and the internet gambling café Tuesdays, Wednesdays, and Thursdays from 3:00 p.m. to 8:00 p.m.

Bruno was still a tough but charming guy who knew how to get what he wanted. He made Nina feel like she was a boss who could do anything she wanted. Bruno had a way with words that spoke directly to Nina's inner soul.

"So, you gon' tell me what's up with li'l man's daddy or what?" Bruno asked Nina as she sat down at the table. She had just gotten back from changing Jacob's diaper.

"Damn. Why you all up in my business?" Nina responded.

"Because I can be all up in yours, that's why," Bruno quickly replied, giving Nina a familiar flirty look.

Nina paused and smiled. She was blushing, something that she hadn't done in a while, and she told him the story of her and Tyrese. "Then when I was about eight months preggers," she finished, "he kicked me out. Said the baby wasn't his and to never contact him again. So I didn't, and that's that." Nina picked up her glass and took a big gulp of water.

Bruno sat back in his chair, a little stunned by what he had just heard. "Damn. That's fucked up. Why did he say the baby wasn't his?" Bruno asked.

Nina shrugged. Bruno didn't believe her, and his face showed it. "Don't look at me like that," Nina said.

"Come on, shorty. It's me. You can't play a playa, and you can't slick a can of paint. I know better. What happened? What you do?"

Nina just shook her head. "I don't know. We were fine that morning. Then that afternoon we weren't."

"Nah. That answer is not gon' fly with me, kid. You a beast in more ways than one. I know you can pick a dude apart piece by piece. Leave him sitting buck-naked in the corner sucking his thumb, trying to figure out where he went wrong in life. Nothing? Yeah, right! Try again, sweetie."

Nina laughed so hard she started choking and gasping for air. Tears were coming out of her eyes. "You are so crazy!" Nina stated to Bruno. "Why would you say something like that?"

"Because that shit is true. What you mean?" Bruno replied. "If you don't want to tell me, just say that. Don't insult my intelligence by trying to serve me that bland, lame-ass 'nothing' as an answer."

Bruno's words were moving Nina's spirit in more ways than one. She caught herself admiring all the things she loved about him. His swag, his smell, his words, and his energy were the things that no woman could deny that Bruno possessed. He always could read Nina like a book, a skill not even Tyrese had mastered.

Bruno could tell that Nina was keeping something from him. It was all over her face and in how she sat with her shoulders hung low. He was about to push a little harder, then decided to just let it go. It had to be deep and really serious for her to try so hard to hide it. He didn't want to ruin their reunion by getting Nina upset.

"You and ya homegirl still rocking, huh? That shit is pretty dope."

"Oh, yeah!" Nina said with much more enthusiasm than when she was telling the story about her and Tyrese. "Rene is my boo for life! She was the only person there for me when Tyrese put me out. I'll do anything for her. I hate her dumb-ass, wack-ass, punk-ass husband though. He could kick rocks with flip-flops on for all I care. If he weren't there, living with Rene and the kids would be perfect."

"Well, shit! What did that nigga do to you?" Bruno said, shocked at how quickly Nina's mood changed.

"He's just not good enough for Rene. She deserves somebody who loves, respects, and supports her the same way she does them. That nigga is weak, irritating, and basically just in the way."

Bruno was a little confused by Nina's last remark, but he didn't say anything or ask her to explain herself.

Rene's great life seemed to be fading slowly away right before her eyes. In the months that followed, things went from dreamy and too good to be true to stressful and incredibly bad in Rene's world.

Her job was going great, but with penalties of course. She was given a nice promotion, which meant more money and a better life for her and her family, but with the money also came more responsibilities, longer days, and later hours. Sometimes she even had to work while she was at home. Not only was she missing her kids, but her marriage seemed to be lacking and at a standstill as well.

Jalen's compliments and warm smiles were coming less and less, along with his affection. When Rene would try to be affectionate with him, he seemed uninterested. He would always turn her away or say he was tired. Even when Rene sneaked in the shower and tried to surprise him with an oral treat, he rejected her and asked if she could just wash his back. In all of their years together, Jalen had never turned down her offers of oral sex.

To add gas to a growing fire, Jalen and Nina were behaving as if they were in a full-fledged war. They would go days without saying a word to each other, and when they finally did talk, it was always an argument filled with yelling, cussing, and horrible insults.

One day, Rene managed to get off work a little early. When she got home, she found Nina in her room bawling her eyes out. This was the second time this had happened.

Nina never had any real explanation as to why she was crying. She attempted to give some weak excuses like it was PMS or she thought that maybe she had failed a test at school. Rene knew better. Nina's behavior was becoming stranger and stranger, and Rene was beginning to worry.

One evening, Rene walked through the garage door, coming home late from work. She bumped into Nina, who was walking around the house in a tank top and some boy-shorts panties. Her ass was literally hanging out of the underwear.

"Are you nuts?" asked Rene aggressively.

Nina looked at Rene with a surprised expression on her face. "What's wrong? What did I do?" she asked.

"Put some damn clothes on! Ain't nobody tipping yo' ass in here. This is not the damn strip club!" Rene reminded Nina.

Nina seemed surprised. Rene had never talked to her like that. "Okay, ReRe. My bad," Nina said somberly. "I mean, I always walk around in my pajamas. Didn't think it was an issue."

Rene was annoyed by Nina's response. "Girl, bye! Those are drawers! Not pajamas. Give me a break! You are grown. You know the difference. Stop with the excuses. Try again!"

Nina apologized once again to Rene and ran upstairs to change. That conversation caused Nina to become a little paranoid. Did Rene know that she was back working at a strip club?

A few weeks had passed, and Nina was in the rhythm of her new schedule. She was paying DJ to keep Jacob at night and telling Rene that she was working for the temp agency again to keep her from getting suspicious. She hated lying, but she had to do what she had to do to keep Rene from being angry with her.

Nina's schedule wasn't the only thing that was changing. Something that had started to happen often and was definitely starting to really bug Rene was Nina's constant questioning about her relationship with Jalen. Sometimes the questions quickly turned into Nina badgering Rene about Jalen's comings and goings. She pleaded with Rene to pay attention and not be stupid. Whenever Jalen and Nina were in the same room the tension and animosity that would be in the air would be so thick you could cut it with a dull knife.

One night, Jalen came into their bedroom steaming mad. He was so pissed at Nina. He started screaming at Rene that Nina had to go. He couldn't stand the sight of her anymore. His explanation for all the anger and constant feuding with Nina was that he was tired of her freeloading and interfering in their marriage. He was ready for her to leave their home.

With Nina being in cosmetology school part-time, braiding hair on the side, and working at what Rene thought was a temp job only making $10 an hour, there was no way Nina could afford a place of her own and daycare for Jacob, especially considering that she was getting no help from Tyrese. Jalen didn't seem to care. All he would ever say was, "Sounds like a personal problem to me. Maybe next time she will keep her nasty legs closed."

"That's not fair, Jay. We said she could stay until she got her license and into a salon," Rene said, trying to remind Jalen of their agreement.

Jalen was not interested. "I'm not trying to hear that shit. I'm tired of looking at her. My patience has run out! She is so disgusting, and I don't want her around."

Rene looked at Jalen with pure confusion on her face. "Disgusting? Don't you think you're being a little dramatic right now? I mean, really?"

Jalen walked out of the bathroom and stood in the entryway. "Are you serious right now?" he firmly asked Rene. "Are you my wife or Nina's? Fuck no, I'm not being dramatic, and I don't like that I have to have this long-ass, repetitive conversation about who can and cannot live in my house!"

Rene tried to reason with Jalen, but it fell on deaf ears. He grabbed a hoodie from the top shelf of their closet and slipped it over his head, then slid his feet into some Nike slide sandals.

"Wait, where are you going?" Rene asked while standing in Jalen's way.

"Move, Rene!" he ordered.

"No!" she snapped. "Not until you tell me where you are going."

"Damn! I'm going over to my cousin Donavan's. Is that okay with you?" Jalen yelled back.

Rene had had enough of the bickering. She slowly slid out of Jalen's way and let him leave. When she heard his truck start and then pull off, she flopped down on her bed and began to cry. Her world was crumbling around her, and she didn't know how to make it stop.

Rene was so perplexed. She did not want to turn her back on her friend, but at the same time, she could not let her friendship with Nina destroy her marriage. Her family and Nina were all she had, and she wasn't ready to lose any of them.

The next night, after they both had calmed down and were watching a movie on TV together, Rene decided to confront Jalen with her feelings and questions.

"Jay, what's really going on?" she asked.

Jalen turned and looked at his wife as if he had no idea what she was talking about. "What do you mean, bae?"

Rene sat up and moved her feet off his lap. "I mean, I know you and Nina have never been the coolest, but you at least got along. You two never had an issue with being cordial to one another. It's so bad now! I'm afraid one day I'm going to come home from work and find one of you physically hurt or dead!"

Jalen shook his head and formed a little grin of empathy. "I know it bothers you that your friend and I don't get along, and I'm sorry about that, but she is a horrible woman. She's a horrible woman who is not as good a friend as you think she is. I'm your husband, and it's my job to protect you physically, mentally, and emotionally. That's all I'm trying to do. I know how much you love Nina. That is the only reason I tolerate her as much as I do, but trust me when I say your love runs a lot deeper for her than her love runs for you."

Rene sat in silence as she listened to her husband. What in the world was going on? *What does Jalen mean by "protect" me? Why on earth would he need to protect me from Nina?*

"Jalen, stop beating around the bush. What does all of this mean? You aren't telling me anything."

Jalen sighed and grabbed Rene's hand. "Just know that your friend is trifling, and no matter what, I love you and I will always have your back."

He kissed Rene's hand and placed it on his face. Tears of frustration started to form in Rene's eyes. She was completely annoyed, frustrated, and irritated all at the same time. The fact that Jalen would not just come out and tell her what he knew and why he felt the way he felt was not making any sense.

Rene pulled her hand away and in a firm voice said to Jalen, "Not good enough!" She jumped up and put on some jeans and a shirt.

"Where are you going? It's eleven o'clock at night, woman!" said Jalen.

Rene looked at him and rolled her eyes. She went to her vanity, washed her face, put on some lip gloss and earrings, and made her way back to the bedroom.

"Rene!" Jalen jumped up and put his arm on the door of their bedroom to keep Rene from opening it. "Where are you going?"

"To clear my head! All you did was make it cloudier than it was, so now I need to relieve some stress. Figure some things out."

"Okay. Okay, I'm sorry, babe. Don't leave. It's too late, and I don't want you out in the world by yourself," pleaded Jalen.

"I'm not trying to hear anything you have to say right now. Move your arm, Jalen. Now!" Rene demanded.

Jalen could tell that Rene meant business. She had a way of letting you know when playtime was over and she was just a few seconds away from switching her words to slaps and punches. Jalen humbly moved his arm and let Rene through.

As Rene made her way to the garage door, she passed Nina in the kitchen fixing something to eat. Nina put down the spoon in her hand to find out what was going on.

"Girl, where are you going? More importantly, where you going without me?" Nina inquired.

"Out! Damn! Is everybody my fucking warden around here?" Rene snapped as she moved quickly toward the door.

"Sorry! What's wrong? Why are you—" Before Nina could finish her sentence, Rene walked out the door and slammed it behind her.

Rene drove around the city, trying to figure out where she could go. She really wasn't a big club person, so that was out of the question. She did not want to go to any hot spots in the city because she and Jalen both knew so many people she did not want to run into any familiar faces and have to put a fake smile on her face.

She decided to drive to the other side of town to a small pub she'd heard her coworkers talking about. She went and sat down at the bar. She ordered a double shot of Patrón with a side of pineapple juice.

I can't believe this crap. Why is Jalen talking in circles and not making any sense? We don't keep secrets from each other. That's not what we do. Why would he need to protect me from Nina? Nina loves me. I trust her. If anybody in this world has my back, it's her. What harm could she do to me?

Rene looked at the menu with a blank face. She wasn't a big burger eater, which was what this pub specialized in. She wasn't quite sure if she was even hungry or if her nerves were shot and she wanted some comfort food. She wanted to be able to drive home, so she definitely needed to put something on her stomach, but not something so heavy it would make her feel sick.

While she pondered the menu, she felt a tap on her shoulder. She turned around and could not believe the figure standing in front of her.

"Hey there, beautiful lady!" said the charming voice to Rene. "It's strange seeing you here! Are you alone?"

Rene sat there in awe. Her mouth was slightly open, yet nothing was coming out. She was stuck.

"Are you okay?" the voice asked.

"Tyrese?" Rene said as her voice cracked.

"Hey, long time no see, stranger. How you been?" he asked.

It took all Rene had in her not to jump up and tackle Tyrese to the floor. *How dare this bum and deadbeat dad come up to me? I should punch this dude in his stupid-ass face.*

"'How you been . . . stranger'?" Rene replied, mocking him. "You have got to be joking, dude! Are you drunk or something? You have got to have some big fucking balls to come up and talk to me like we are old friends after the way you did my girl. Are you crazy? How about instead of saying, 'Hey, old stranger,' you try asking how your son is doing? Ask me if I have any pictures of him that you can see. Try asking that!"

Tyrese just shook his head. "I can see you are still caught up in the black widow's web of lies and deceit."

"Caught up in what? You need to tread very lightly talking about my friend. I would hate to embarrass you in front of all these people!" she snapped at Tyrese.

Tyrese just sighed and shrugged. "Look, Rene, I always thought you were a real cool chick and had a good head on your shoulders, so I'm going to go out on a limb and share something with you. Don't let Nina fool you. She is flat-out one of the worst human beings I have ever met in my life! I'm sure she made me out to be some hard-core villain who cares nothing about her or the baby. Deep down inside, I think you know me better than that. That's not the case at all. Your girl is not who or what you think she is."

Rene was starting to feel pressure in her chest. Her heart was racing. For the second time in one evening, she was hearing the same awful things about Nina. However, Rene always considered the source when she received information. How valid was it coming from Tyrese? After all, he did put Nina out while she was pregnant with his baby, and he had not been taking care of his son at all.

"You know what, Tyrese? Save it! You're not about to turn me against my best friend because you can't step up to the plate!" Rene said as she turned her back to Tyrese.

"No, no, no, baby girl. You got it all wrong!" replied Tyrese as he turned Rene's barstool back around to face him. "I'm not trying to turn you against her, but I bet all the money in my savings account that as soon as you find out the truth about her, no one will have to turn you against her, because she turned against you first."

"What in the hell are you talking about?" Rene snapped. "Don't come at me with all this nonsense like that's not my best friend! We have known each other for over twenty years. In that time, she has never done anything to hurt me, and she never will do anything to hurt me. You're just trying to start some shit just like the weak-ass man you are! I see right through your tired ass. Get your punk ass out of my face, Tyrese!" Rene demanded.

Tyrese looked at Rene and leaned in close as he held his arm on the top of her barstool. "Rene, you are a beautiful person. You deserve a better friend, and I really do hope one day that you get it. To be completely honest and transparent, I also hope that one day I can show you what it means to be treated like the loving and loyal woman you are. Until that day comes, you take care of yourself, and watch your back."

Rene looked Tyrese directly in his eyes. "I suggest you get your arm from around my chair and get out of my face before I slap fire out of you!" Rene whispered angrily to Tyrese, talking through her teeth.

Tyrese slowly backed away with a sarcastic smirk on his face. "Have a good evening, Rene." He turned and went to a table in the back of the pub.

If Rene had not been confused before, she definitely was now. What was all this bullshit about Nina? How could she be a bad person?

I mean, I've seen her about to fight a 300-pound chick before to defend me. Jalen and Tyrese are tripping. They are just jealous of our relationship. Especially Tyrese. He had a lot of nerve to come over here and try to make Nina out to be a bad person. Nina is a great mother and a great friend. He needs to shut the hell up talking that crazy talk!

Rene sat there trying to figure what she should do. How should she handle the load of madness that was just dumped in her lap? She decided to order a margarita and nachos.

As she ate and drank, she could not stop wondering about Nina and the shots that both Jalen and Tyrese were taking at her. What could she possibly be doing? *This is not right!* The pit of her stomach began to ball up and turn over. She began to feel nauseated. She didn't know if she should mention any of this to Nina or just ignore it. *If I do say something to her, what would I say? "Why is your deadbeat baby daddy telling me you are a crazy person and trifling? Oh, yeah, and Jalen, the person who probably hates you more than Tyrese, why is he saying that you're no good and a fake-ass, horrible friend?"* That just was not the way to come at your girl without hurting her feelings.

Rene finished her drink and food, got in her car, and drove around a little bit longer. Her mind was too unstable to go home right away.

When she finally did make it home, Nina was up waiting for her.

"Girl, you all right?" Nina asked. "I was texting you, calling you, and you didn't answer your phone at all. What's wrong?"

Rene tried to open her mouth, but she could not talk. Nothing was coming out. She just started to bawl her eyes out.

"Oh, my goodness!" Nina jumped up and gave Rene a hug. "Girl, what is the matter? Talk to me! Did someone hurt you? What happened? You know I'm here for you!"

Rene decided not to confront Nina or even bring it up. "It's nothing," she replied through her tears. "My job is just stressing me out, and I can't really be the type of mom I want to be for my kids. It's just becoming too much!"

"Don't you worry about that! You are a great mom, a great wife, and a great friend. If anybody tells you different, you just tell them to come and see me," Nina assured Rene as she tried to make light of the situation in an effort to cheer Rene up.

"I'm gonna go in here and make you one of my specialty drinks. I know you don't drink a lot, and from the looks of it, you've probably had enough for the night, but trust me, Nina's Ass Kicker will get you right in no time! You'll have a smile so big on your face your cheeks are gonna be hurting."

Rene just sat on the couch in dismay, trying to sort out everything floating around in her head. *Lord, please don't let this stuff about my friend be true. I don't know if I can handle it. If it is true, God, please give me the strength and the calmness to deal with it without going to jail. Amen.*

Chapter 4

The Truth?

Days and weeks passed by, and Rene was no less confused than she was when she had her initial conversation with Jalen. The thoughts that sometimes ran through her head sent her on an emotional roller coaster. She would break down and just sob uncontrollably. Other times she would be so angry she wanted to punch the wall. One minute she was mad, and the next she would be so depressed she would start to feel sick. She dived headfirst into her work to help ease her discomfort and occupy her thoughts. She volunteered to work overtime and travel to different cities, and she even worked on the weekends.

If she didn't have to work, she would take the kids and go somewhere, anywhere, just to be out of the house and not have to deal with or look at Nina or Jalen. She had reached a point of panic and felt like she was a stranger in her own home. The feelings of discomfort and not trusting Jalen or Nina grew bigger and bigger with each day that passed. It was hard for Rene to function sometimes. She often felt alone and as though she had no one to trust, turn to, or depend on. It was a feeling that was causing Rene to become emotionally exhausted and mentally drained.

One night, Rene made plans to come home a little early. She knew that Nina would be out late because she was working. Jalen had sent her a text earlier in the day saying that he was giving a quote on a job that was three hours away, meaning he would be home later than usual. Her kids were on break from school and spending the week with her mom. Rene would have the house all to herself, something that hardly ever happened. She desperately needed this mental break.

"Finally I can enjoy my home in peace!" she said to herself as she slipped her heels off her feet.

She ran a tub of water, adding lavender oil and bubble bath to help her relax. Rene then turned on some smooth music and let her muscles rest and her tensions melt away in the warm, bubble-filled bath. She allowed her mind to drift to a time when life was easy and made sense.

She remembered the times when she and Jalen were dating and he was all she wanted and more. He always had his shortcomings, but overall, he was an incredible guy. Everything made so much sense back then. Now it was almost like she did not know who Jalen was. It was like he had turned into this new man and forgotten to tell her.

First it was school and then football that seemed to interfere with their relationship. Then his business became the thing that kept Rene from enjoying the fullness of her marriage. Once that was under control, Rene's job seemed to be the hurdle in their way, and now there was this "secret" that nobody felt was important enough to share with Rene. It was making her feel as though she were the one in the wrong, like she had committed some type of violation and now she was being punished for it. It was almost as if she was not number one anymore.

As Rene continued to enjoy her bath and allow her body to relax, it dawned on her that it had been a while since she had been pleased sexually. A nice, hard orgasm always had a way of relaxing Rene and easing any tension she was experiencing.

She lifted her leg out of the water and allowed it to rest on the edge of the tub. Water ran down her foot and dripped on the floor. She turned on the jets in her Jacuzzi tub and maneuvered her body to a position that would allow the fast, forceful stream of warm water to beat against her throbbing love box. She then began to rub her clit with the tips of her index and middle fingers, enjoying the feeling of arousal that she was experiencing. A warm sensation was forming in her abdomen and beginning to spread throughout her body. The arousing sensation was becoming more intense. Right before she reached her climax, she heard a quiet yet familiar voice whisper, "Hey, baby. Would you like some help with that?"

Rene opened her eyes, startled to find Jalen standing in the doorway of the bathroom. He was shirtless and starting to unbuckle his pants.

"Damn it! Would you get out and leave me alone?" Rene yelled at Jalen. "Shit! Can I do anything in peace? Stop bothering me, Jay."

"Don't be like that, sweetie," begged Jalen. "At least let me wash your back," he said eagerly as he reached for Rene's loofah.

"No, thank you!" Rene answered quickly. "What are doing here? I thought you had an out-of-town job."

"I did," answered Jalen. "We finished early, and I called your office, but Amy said you headed home early. With the kids gone, I figured I'd surprise you. What's wrong? I can't come home now?"

"Nothing is wrong. I just wanted to be alone," snapped Rene.

Jalen walked over to the tub and sat on the floor next to it. He wanted to make sure he would be face-to-face with Rene. "Come on now. How long have we been together? I feel you when you walk in the room, even if there are five hundred other people around us. I feed off of your energy. We are soulmates. You don't think I know when something is wrong with you? So come on, spill it! Tell me what's wrong with my queen," pushed Jalen.

Rene closed her eyes and took a deep breath. Even though she did not want to talk because her spirit was so beat up and exhausted, she knew she could not avoid her husband and this situation any longer. He was right. No matter what she said or did, he would know if something was off. He always did.

"Okay. Jay, this whole feud and secret thing going on between you and Nina is taking a toll on me. I don't know if I'm coming or going. I'm having breakdowns in the middle of the day. On one hand, I feel like I'm a stranger in my own house. On the other hand, I feel like the people closest to me are total strangers. I feel like I don't even know who you two are anymore."

"Why would you feel like that?" asked Jalen.

Rene looked at Jalen with frustration in her eyes. "What kind of question is that? Why do you think? There is obviously something big that happened that is causing you and Nina to behave the way you are," Rene explained. "I'm the only one who doesn't know what it is. Then I bumped into Tyrese, and he starts telling me—"

"Tyrese?" Jalen interrupted. "Where did you see him, and what did he say to you?" Jalen's tone changed, and his voice seemed to indicate that he was anxious. His excitement caught Rene off guard. He almost had a bit of nervousness in his voice.

"I mean, pretty much the same thing you said," Rene answered. "He said that Nina wasn't all she's cracked up to be. He said that she was not a good person or a good friend. He said I should watch my back. What does everyone seem to know that I don't? Why won't anyone just tell me what Nina did that would classify her as a bad friend? Everyone seems to be so concerned about my well-being, but no one wants to tell me anything. I'm not a kid or some fragile person. It's not right and it's not fair. How am I supposed to protect myself when I have no clue what I'm protecting myself from?"

By this time, Rene was no longer relaxing in her bathwater but sitting straight up with tears rolling down her face. The more she talked, the more excited and angrier she became.

Jalen's heart melted. He loved Rene so much, and he hated to see her torn up like this. He stared at her as she spoke to him. Jalen just wanted to take her in his arms and tell her that everything was going to be okay. In the midst of feeling sorry for Rene, Jalen could not help but notice the water rolling off her body, giving her a glow that enhanced her beauty and features.

Bubbles slowly glided down her arm and off her breast into the water. She had such a beautiful face and breathtaking eyes. Jalen suddenly noticed that he was not paying attention to what his wife was saying but becoming turned on by her beauty. He wasn't ignoring her on purpose. It was the effect she had on him. All the years they had been together did not decrease the level of attraction he had for her. If anything, their time together had intensified it.

He snapped out of his daydream just in time to hear and feel the pain and anguish in Rene's voice. All this time, he thought that by not telling Rene any details regarding Nina and her jacked-up ways, he was protecting her feelings. Now he could see that the reality of the situation was he was inflicting the very pain that he was trying to shield her from.

"Okay, Rene. Okay. You win. I will tell you whatever it is you think you need to know. Whatever will take that pain out of your eyes, I'll say it," Jalen said as he grabbed a towel to dry Rene off. He helped her out of the tub, wrapped her wet body in the towel, and escorted her to their bedroom.

Jalen stood Rene in front of him and began to dry her off. Rene, still very much irritated with Jalen, snatched the towel from his hands. "I got it," she said as she finished getting all of the water off her body.

She wrapped herself up in the towel, and they both sat down on the bed. Jalen wrapped his arm around her waist and pulled her closer to him. Jalen tried to gaze into Rene's eyes, but she wouldn't allow it. Rene was not in denial about the love she had for her husband even in the midst of all the confusion. She was not trying to get caught up in his spell or mesmerized by his charm. Rene knew that what Jalen was about to tell her had the potential to change her life forever. She was ready to hear it. The frustration and anxiety she had been going through had pretty much prepared her for anything.

"Do you remember about a year or so ago," Jalen started, "when I went to the city for Donavan's bachelor party?"

"I remember," Rene replied.

"While we were at Flood's, I bumped into Nina. We said what's up and kicked it for a bit. She was with some other chicks, and of course, I was with all the fellas."

As Jalen was talking, Rene's heart started beating 200 beats a minute. She had no idea where this story was going, and all the possibilities were starting to scare her.

"After a couple of laughs, Nina and I parted ways," Jalen continued. "Later on that night, me and the fellas bumped into Nina and the chick she was with earlier, I think her name is Shanequa, again at the strip club."

As soon as Rene heard that name, she knew this story was going to get ugly.

"You know how crazy Nina and her girl can be. They started flirting and dancing around us. It was cool. I wasn't tripping, because at first, they really weren't paying me any attention. I figured it was because of you, and that shit would have been super weird and awkward. After they got a few lap dances in, they convinced us to let them come along to the next spot. To allow them to keep hanging with us. Of course, I instantly thought they were just trying to use us to get free drinks and food. I tried to warn everybody and tell them how these chicks got down, but they let them come with us anyway. The night went on as planned. We were partying and drinking, bar and club hopping, and just having a good time."

Rene was becoming irritated with Jalen. All of his blabbering and unnecessary details were becoming too much. She felt like he was attempting to stall. Before she knew it, she yelled out, "Would you stop bullshitting around and get to the damn point?"

Her outburst startled Jalen and made him jump a little. Jalen sat back in shock, slightly concerned. The tone of Rene's voice made him feel like she might be close to slugging him in the face. Rene didn't curse very often. That accompanied by the tone of her voice was something new to Jalen, and he was not prepared to receive it.

"All right! All right! I'm sorry. I'm just trying to help you get the whole picture. That's all, babe," Jalen explained, holding his hands up to show he did not want any trouble with Rene. Jalen put his arm back around Rene's waist, and she quickly removed it and gave him a cold and serious look.

"Okay, so we're at this club called Hangovers, sitting in one of the VIP booths. It was a little packed in there, so I made sure I went straight to the booth and sat down. I wanted to be comfortable. I starting smoking hookah, sipping on my drink, and just vibing to the music. A few minutes later, Nina comes over. She moved my arm, and she sat on my lap. I didn't say anything at first. Like I said, it was a little packed in there. There really wasn't anywhere to sit. We had all been drinking, and I figured Nina didn't want to stand up. But then . . ." Jalen paused. His eyes began to bounce from the floor to the ceiling. It was almost as if he didn't want to talk because he was afraid of getting in trouble. Like a kid or something.

"Then what?" Rene asked Jalen out of frustration.

Jalen sighed. "While she was sitting on my lap, she started rubbing my hair and talking about my waves and my line-up. I was for the most part ignoring her. Again, we had all been drinking, so I wasn't giving it much energy. Then this crazy broad started grinding on my lap and doing all these stripper-type dance moves. I was shell-shocked. I literally just sat there with my arms open, unable to say anything. Just stuck! I couldn't believe she was doing what she was doing. Once I snapped out of it, I pushed her off me. I told her to take her drunk ass somewhere else with that bullshit."

Jalen paused in his story long enough to get a look at Rene's face. It clearly was saying, "I don't believe you."

"I did, bae. I promise I did! I really did push her off of me!" Jalen pleaded with Rene, trying his hardest to get that look off of her face.

"Just keep going, Jalen!" demanded Rene.

Jalen did as he was told. "No matter what I did or what I said, she wouldn't stop! She kept trying to get back on my lap. First backward, you know, with her back to my face. Then she tried to straddle me! She was putting her titties in my face, and the entire time, I'm blocking her with my forearm. I keep repeating to the girl to get off of me. Begging her to go harass someone else. All of a sudden, she started trying to grab my dick. I'm screaming, telling her to stop, steady trying to cover my shit and keep her away from it. She just laughed like it was nothing. I mean, it was crazy. Like she was possessed! To add insult to injury, Nina started saying stuff like, 'Rene don't know what she got in you. I could teach you a thing or two. Rene so stuck up, y'all probably only do it missionary style.' Shit had me all fucked up in the head. What really blew me back was when she said, 'Her head game is not as tight as mine.' Then she grabbed my face with both of her hands, and she kissed me! I'm not talking about a quick, light peck. She was really trying to give me a passionate, intimate kiss, with tongue and all! At this point I'm boiling inside. I jumped up, and I knocked her off of me. She fell down and hit the floor pretty hard. Everyone started making their way back to the booth. Security and my boys were all looking at me like I'm crazy and trying to figure out why I knocked Nina on the floor."

Rene was absolutely speechless. If Nina weren't her best friend, the story wouldn't be so bad. It wouldn't have hurt her heart and her feelings the way it did. Rene had dealt with women throwing themselves at Jalen when they were in college. Those stories were something that never really got her worked up. Jalen always came and told her, so she never was caught off guard by a chick and her shenanigans. This of course was way different. Nina wasn't just some chick. She was family.

Everything inside of Rene felt like it was balled up and on fire. She was so angry she probably could have kicked down a brick wall. She couldn't believe what Jalen had told her, and she was in disbelief that his story wasn't finished. He still had more to say.

"I started telling everyone that she is crazy. 'Don't look at me. Look at her!' Nina starts crying. Fake tears to me. Shit meant nothing to me. The more she kept saying that she was sorry and that she didn't mean it, the more pissed I got. All that drunk talk was not flying with me. I know her. I know bullshit when I see it. She knew exactly what she was doing.

"Everyone started helping her up, and we all went back to the party bus to head home. Again, I'm sitting there minding my own business, trying to keep my cool and not let the bitch ruin my night. I look up and here she comes. She sits down next to me and puts her hand on my thigh. Nina starts telling me she was sorry about what she did in the club, but she meant what she said. I look at her like, what the fuck? She proceeds to tell me how much she really has been feeling me but never said anything because she wasn't sure how I would react. The entire time she's talking, I'm thinking, *you could not pay me to touch this skanky bitch with another man's dick!*

"I asked her to get away from me, but she just kept coming at me so damn hard! I'm doing all I can to get her out of my face, and then I look over, and Shanequa is giving Mark and Shawn head at the same time while Benny's dumb ass is fingering her pussy! Right there in front of everybody on the bus! Then Nina's trifling ass leans over and says in my ear, 'You want me to show you just how good my head game is? You could be getting exactly what your boys are getting. I know Rene stuck-up ass not sucking it right, if she sucking it at all! You can cum in mouth and everything. I'll swallow all them seeds for your fine ass.'

"I lost it, Rene! I pushed Nina so hard her back slammed against the back of the bus. I stood up and smacked the shit out of Nina and cursed her out like she was a nigga who stole from me."

Rene closed her eyes and started thinking back to that time frame. She remembered meeting Nina at the nail salon and her having a nasty bruise on her face. Rene's eyes instantly started to fill with tears. "I remember . . ." she started to share.

"You remember what, baby?" Jalen asked. He could see the tears very close to falling from Rene's eyes. He put his arms around her shoulders to offer her some comfort.

"I remember when that happened. We were getting our nails done, and I saw this nasty bruise on her face. When I asked her about it, she told me she slipped getting out of the shower and hit her face on the floor. I knew she was lying. I thought that Nina and Tyrese must've gotten into a fight or something, and she was trying to cover for him. She had done that before with a different boyfriend. She looked me dead in my face and lied. Like it was nothing."

Rene began to sob uncontrollably. What had Jalen just told her? She felt like she was having a bad dream and couldn't wake up. Her head was so cluttered and overflowing with emotions and random thoughts. She didn't know how to react, what to do, what to say, or what to think.

Jalen could not stand the awkward silence that filled the room. "I'm sorry, babe!" Jalen blurted out. "I really am. I wanted to tell you, but Nina called me the next day and begged me not to say anything to you. She apologized and said she was just drunk and didn't mean any of it. I cursed her out again, this time even worse than before. All she said was she understood my anger and hoped that I could forgive her. She tried to assure me that she'd had too much to drink and something like that would never happen again. I said bullshit! You know my philosophy, baby. Like my mama used to say, a drunk mouth speaks a sober heart!"

"Why didn't you tell me?" Rene yelled at Jalen as she jumped up off of their bed.

Jalen tried to stay calm when he answered her. "I didn't want to hurt you. As horrible as Nina is, I know how you feel about her! I wanted to protect you!" Jalen said as he tried to grab Rene's hand. She quickly pulled it away.

"Protect *me?*" Rene asked. "Or are you protecting yourself? Are you sure you're telling me the whole story and not your version of the story? Telling me the parts that make you look good and Nina look bad all by herself? It's funny how Nina did all these horrible acts of betrayal and you were the innocent victim throughout the entire ordeal."

Jalen stood up and walked toward Rene. "Are you trying to tell me that your love for that nasty, trifling, ugly-ass trick runs deeper than your love and trust for me? I did exactly what you asked me to do. I swallowed my pride, I manned up, even broke guy code to tell you exactly what went down that night, and you turn around and show your appreciation by questioning me about it?"

"I don't know what to think!" Rene snapped at him as she put lotion on. "This is all just too much for me! It's overwhelming. You have got to realize that."

"I love you!" Jalen pleaded. "I would never do anything to intentionally hurt you! Don't you know that? I'm sorry I didn't tell you right away, but I didn't want to see that look of disappointment and hurt in your eyes. The one that you have right now!"

Rene grabbed a black duffel bag out of the closet. She began to stuff it with a few of her belongings. She was crying so hard that tears were beginning to fall into the bag.

"Wait! Why are you packing? No! No way! You can't leave!" Jalen insisted.

"Move, Jalen!" Rene demanded. "I can't stay here with you. It would not be a wise thing to do for you or me. I have to go!"

"No, Rene! We are going to talk about this! We can't fix this and move on with our lives if you walk away." Jalen's voice began to crack as if he was going to break down at any moment. "Please just wait. Don't go! Just calm down and think."

Rene acted as if Jalen was not saying anything at all. She dropped her toiletries case into the bag, zipped it up, and headed for the bedroom door.

Jalen dropped to his knees and grabbed Rene by her legs. He started to cry as his pleas for Rene to not leave began to sound more and more desperate.

Rene's heart ached. She was lost, confused, and angry, and she wasn't sure if she could separate her feelings at that moment. She loved Jalen with all her heart. She always thought that no matter what transpired between them, she would want her marriage to work. Now she wasn't so sure.

The images that were playing over and over in her head of Jalen and Nina together hurt like hell. Despite the pain she was feeling, her love for Jalen stirred up some compassion from deep inside of her. Her love allowed his pleas to pierce her heart whether she liked it or not. As badly as she wanted to leave, she knew that leaving would break Jalen, and she didn't want to hurt him. She couldn't live with the thought that she'd inflicted that type of pain on him.

Rene inhaled a deep breath and released it. She looked down at her tearful husband and shook her head. She laid her hand on Jalen's head and dropped her duffel bag onto the floor.

Chapter 5

Me, He, and She

When Rene opened her red and puffy eyes, it took her a moment to think about where she was. The night before seemed so unreal. Her first thought was that the entire thing was just a dream. However, when she tried to roll over and couldn't because Jalen was lying on her stomach, the harsh reality began to set in, and she knew that everything that had taken place was definitely her fucked-up reality. It was also something that she was going to have to deal with one way or another. She slowly tried to wiggle unnoticed from under Jalen's grip, but it didn't work.

"Good morning, beautiful," said Jalen, his voice scratchy from just waking up.

"Good morning," Rene softly replied. "Can you get up please? I have to use the bathroom, and you lying on my stomach is starting to hurt."

Jalen moved over and allowed Rene to get out of bed. As Rene walked to the bathroom, tears started to fall from her eyes, and she didn't even know why. For the first time ever, Jalen made Rene's skin crawl, and she did not want him to touch her. Maybe it was all the uncertainty in her life when everything was so definite before. Maybe it was the lingering frustration from knowing that the trust she had in her marriage was now gone. Knowing Jalen was capable of keeping secrets from her for such a long period of time killed it.

Rene kept repeating in her head that if Nina were just some girl off the street, or a woman she knew casually and was kind of cool with, Rene wouldn't have been so upset. She and Jalen had been together for a long time. She had gone through her share of groupies and accusations. She was never threatened by any of them. Not ever. Those types of women and situations were just a part of life as far as Rene was concerned. It was the price she'd pay to be with a man like Jalen.

He was a charming and attractive guy. She was used to women being aggressive and doing everything they could to catch his eye and get his attention. She had even experienced Jalen having a stalker and needing a restraining order against a girl from his old neighborhood. Rene had definitely had her share of "the other woman" moments, but this was totally different and not even close in comparison.

This aggressive chick was Nina: her friend, her sister, a person she adored and trusted with her life. The person who loved and cared for her children as if they were her own. How could she do and say those things to Jalen, then come and smile in her face? Even if she was drunk, why would those thoughts even be on her brain?

There was something about this story that still wasn't sitting well with Rene. Although Jalen's story was not completely farfetched, it seemed to have some holes. Rene could not say why she felt the way she did. Call it woman's intuition or God Himself whispering in her ear. Whatever it was, it had her all worked up, and it would not let her mind rest.

I'll get to the bottom of this mess! I'm going to do it my way. That I can guarantee and put money on!

As she walked out of the bathroom and back into the bedroom, Jalen was sitting on the edge of the bed, perked up like he had already had twelve cups of coffee.

"Okay, what will it be?" Jalen asked with a huge Kool-Aid smile on his face.

"What will what be?" Rene replied with no emotion at all.

"Breakfast! What do you want for breakfast?" he responded. "You can have whatever you want. I'll cook it, I'll buy it, whatever. It doesn't matter."

Rene squinted and gave Jalen a dumbfounded look. "What, you think you can just feed me, smile while doing a song and dance, and everything will be okay? You thought if you get me nice and full that I would just forget about everything that was said last night?"

"No. I mean, I just thought—" Jalen stammered.

"No! Don't think!" Rene quickly interrupted. "You are not running this show. I am! Just because I didn't leave last night doesn't mean that I won't today or tomorrow. Please don't think I'm taking this shit lightly, because I am not!"

Rene washed her face, brushed her teeth, and got herself dressed. She was on a mission, one that she was determined to complete.

Jalen sat clueless on the bed. He was as lost as a kid in a shopping mall looking for his parents. What had he done? Jalen thought that by coming clean with Rene, she would see Nina for the fucked-up person she was, revealing who he had known for so long she was. He figured Rene would put Nina out, cut all ties with her, and they would move on with their lives. That didn't seem to be the case.

Rene seemed like she wanted more from him. Like she was looking for something that wasn't there or that Jalen hadn't the power to provide. She doubted what he said and questioned his honesty. All Jalen could think was, *how can she not trust me? How can she not believe me? It's not me. It's Nina!*

"Bae. What are you doing? Come on, man. Can we at least talk about this?" asked Jalen.

"Honestly?" Rene said with her back to him. "I'm not in the mood to talk to you right now. I will see you when I see you."

Rene quickly threw her hair in a ponytail, threw on some jeans and some tennis shoes, and walked out to her car. As she pulled out of the driveway, she paused. *Where am I going?* Her mom and kids were having a great time visiting family, making cupcakes, and doing all the wonderful things her mom used to do with her when she was a little girl. Rene didn't want to ruin their fun, being depressed, making her mom sad by dumping all of her emotional baggage on her shoulders.

She was not close enough with any of her other friends to share her personal business with them, especially of this magnitude.

Rene's siblings were all married with families of their own except for her oldest sister, but she did not live in the same city. Even if she could talk to them, Rene would not have told them about her situation. They could not stand Nina and were always looking for any reason to get in her face or put hands on her. They were a lot more aggressive and quick-tempered than Rene was, and they were also very protective of each other. They would have instantly been ready to beat the crap out of Nina and Jalen without hesitation, so visiting them or calling them was not an option either.

"I'll just go shopping, damn it!" she decided. "I deserve it!"

As Rene headed thirty miles north to the outlet mall, she began to question herself. How was she going to face Nina? She was due back home later that day, and Rene had not once given any thought to what she would say or do once she saw her.

"She's going to get the hell outta my house, that's for sure," Rene confirmed to herself. She wasn't sure how she could put Nina out with the baby. Jacob was her godson, and it was her job to make sure he was safe no matter what went on between her and his mom.

Rene decided to shop, eat, and enjoy herself. She treated herself to a pedicure and a manicure and even went to get her hair done. Being that all of those things were her favorites, she hoped they would help ease her mind and relieve some stress.

On the way home from her day of shopping and pampering, Rene concocted a plan of her own to get to the bottom of this whole situation. Was Nina as bad as Jalen made her seem, or was Jalen covering up for some indiscretions of his own?

After I'm done, the truth shall set us all free! Rene proclaimed in her thoughts.

When she returned home, Rene did not see Jalen's truck or Nina's car, so she knew that she would be by herself. She went upstairs, put all of her bags away, and lay down to take a nap. If her plan was going to work, she was going to need all of her energy. She was still a little out of it from the night before.

"I'm hooommme!" yelled a ratchet, high-pitched voice.

Rene slowly opened her eyes. Her heart beat a little faster. She said a quick prayer and sat up in her bed. "Let the games begin," she said to herself.

"Hey, girl, where you at?" Nina yelled through the house.

"I'm upstairs," Rene yelled back as she slipped her sweatshirt on over her head.

Nina came up the stairs and went straight to Rene's room.

"Hey, where's the baby?" questioned Rene.

"Aw, girl, he's with my cousin Sheca!" replied Nina.

"Why is he with Sheca?" Rene asked, confused.

"Her youngest son is having a birthday party, and she wanted Jacob to come. Plus, she has been calling me for over a month, bugging me to let her keep him. I had a long night, so I finally gave in. I didn't feel like being bothered with all those bad-ass kids, so I came home," Nina explained. "I figured if Jacob was over there, then me and you could go hang out and do something. Since I've started working again, we haven't seen each other much. I know you just miss me so much! I dropped him off and came straight here."

Nina plopped down on the bed with her friend. "What's been up? I'm surprised you're here and not out working today. Yo' ass has been working so much."

"Nah, not today. I needed a break. Needed to clear my mind. I decided to have a Rene Only Day. You know, some me time," Rene answered.

"Oh, okay! Wait a minute. Bitch, is that a Gucci bag I see? Oh, I know you didn't go shopping without your girl. That is so messed up, ReRe. You couldn't wait a couple hours and take me with you? That is messed up! Did you at least bring me back a T-shirt?" asked Nina, rolling around on the bed being overly dramatic, trying to get Rene to laugh.

Rene chuckled. "Nope. Sorry. I didn't bring you back a T-shirt. I didn't bring you back a pair of pants, some shoes, or anything like that. You know what I might have for you though?" questioned Rene.

Nina shook her head. "I didn't see a fine brother sitting on the couch when I came in, so nope, I don't know."

"I might have a good, old-fashioned ass whoopin' waiting for you. Now that, I'm pretty sure I can get for you! I know for a fact I have about four or five of them still in me, just waiting to be handed out to someone well deserving," Rene revealed.

Nina stopped laughing and looked at Rene. She realized that she was not smiling at all. She seemed to be furious. "Ass whoopin'? You wanna fight me? What the hell is wrong with you? I'm lost. You wanna fill me in and tell me what this is all about?" Nina asked, stunned at what she just heard Rene say.

"Explain something to me please," Rene began. "Why is it that all of a sudden everyone around me is telling me how bad a friend and woman you are?"

"Whoa, whoa, whoa, Rene. Slow your roll. Who the fuck is everybody? How you gonna come at me like this?" Nina questioned. "You know me better than that! As much shit as you and I have been through. As many times as I've had your back? You really believing the streets now?" Nina asked with an attitude.

Rene stood up from her bed, bent over, and looked Nina dead in her eyes. "If it were the 'streets' doing the talking, we wouldn't even be having this conversation!" Rene stated firmly.

"Who the hell is it then?" Nina asked.

"Your biggest fans. Jalen and Tyrese," answered Rene.

"Oh, hell no!" Nina jumped up, swinging her arms dramatically, pacing back and forth. She was putting on quite a show. "You gonna believe what them dirty muthafuckas have to say about me? You believe what you hear out of their mouths without even checking with your girl? Their shit is just golden now? Come on, for real? What the fuck is going on? Straight up? Since when is that how you and me operate, ReRe?"

Nina's ninja moves and exaggerated movements were not moving Rene emotionally at all. She was used to see her perform. "First of all, relax with all that dramatic shit you doing. That crap don't work on me. Secondly, Jalen is my husband, you crazy lady," Rene explained. "Why wouldn't I trust him? Why wouldn't his word hold a lot of weight with me? Lastly, the things he told me yesterday about you . . . yeah, I wouldn't put them past you at all, Nina. Everything sounds like some foul shit that you would do. Before you go into victim mode, please keep in mind that I know you and how you move better than anyone else."

"Oh, really? Hmmm," Nina said as she sat back down on the corner of the bed. "Well, please enlighten me. What exactly is it that your honorable and wonderful husband told you about me?"

As Rene told Nina the story of the lap dance, the kiss, and the proposition of oral sex, Nina's mouth dropped to the floor.

"As long as I've known you, you have never been so drunk that you started acting crazy. You don't believe in getting that drunk. 'Drunk head fucks up the money.' Remember? That used to be one of your favorite ho quotes," Rene reminded Nina.

"This shit is crazy!" Nina responded. Her eyes were wide, and her mouth was hanging open.

"Don't look so shook, my dear," Rene continued. "You thought I forgot about that shit, didn't you?"

"I didn't mean to get drunk," Nina began to explain. "I was drinking Hennessy, and then somebody bought a whole bunch of tequila shots. Mixing that light and dark liquor like that had me so messed up."

"Damn, you're good. You're quick with lies, too," Rene congratulated Nina. "Always got an explanation for everything. It's pathetic! Like I said, the shit that Jalen said to me was not beyond you or anything you haven't done before. I've heard several stories of your adventures in Ho-ville."

"That dirty, no-good nigga is a lying bastard!" replied Nina. "I don't care what my past is, I'm telling you it's not true. You are killing me right now. I never thought you would be someone who would throw old shit in my face like this. I don't care that Jalen is your husband. He is a bald-faced liar! That night did not go down like that. Okay, yes! I acted somewhat out of character, and I did a few things that were disrespectful to you, and that's my bad on that. But Jalen got the story all twisted up. Maybe he was drunker than he remembers, but shit did not go down the way he said it did."

Rene sat back down on her bed and propped herself up with her pillows. She shook her head in disappointment. "Wow. How did I know you were going to say that?" Rene asked.

Nina looked at Rene in disbelief. "What in the hell is that supposed to mean?"

Rene paused and looked at Nina. "It means exactly what the fuck I said!" Rene yelled, growing more and more upset. "Let me calm down, because I'm not about to sweat out my hair for you. You know what? There's nothing else for us to say. I'm not in the mood to listen to bullshit all over again only to have to listen to it for a third time later. Let's just wait for Jalen to get home. Then we can all sit down and have a wonderful conversation together. Air everything out at one time with everyone at the table. Sounds good?"

Nina quickly changed the subject without answering Rene's question. "Are you going to share with me what you were doing talking to Tyrese? You believe that no-good deadbeat-ass daddy and what he has to say about me too? The one who put me out on the street and won't take care of his own son? Now his word is stronger than mine? I cannot figure out how we got here. Why are you sneaking around behind my back now? When and where did all this talking take place?"

"Bitch, I'm not going to keep telling you to watch your mouth!" said Rene in a cynical tone. She was becoming obviously annoyed with Nina's tone. "I am really starting to believe that you have lost your goddamn mind. All I said was that he told me you weren't as good a friend as I thought you were. Nobody is sneaking doing nothing. In case you forgot, I'm grown! I do what I want, when I want! The last time I checked, you have no authority over me, thus there is no need for me to sneak and do any fucking thing!" Rene affirmed.

"You questioning me about stuff that he said to you is not cool. Grown or not!" snapped Nina.

"Wrong, Nina!" Rene corrected her. "It is cool if the shit is true. From the looks of your reaction, it probably is. You are really worked up to be so fucking innocent. Why is it that people seem to know you better than I, but you and I are supposed to be thicker than thick? Who are you wearing a mask for? Me or them?"

Nina couldn't even look at Rene anymore. She fought back the tears that were forming. She could not believe that this was happening. The friendship that she had worked so hard to build and maintain all these years, doing all that she could to hold it together, was slipping away.

"Since you're already pissed at me, I should just keep the party going. I might as well put it all out there so I don't get accused of anything else," Nina started to share.

"Say what? What the hell are you talking about now?" Rene asked, confused.

"The new job I have is not working for no dumb-ass temp agency. I started working for Bruno again."

Rene's eyes got big as she turned and looked at Nina. "What? Are you serious? You're back dancing again?"

"No. I'm not!" Nina quickly corrected her. "I'm the manager of his club and gambling spot. I handle all the books, and all the employees report to me. You do know I'm good at more than shaking my ass, right? That's just one of my moneymaking skills. The pay is good, and I'm a boss! I get respect. Nobody messes with me."

Rene laughed hysterically. "Don't give yourself so much credit. If it were all roses and rainbows, you wouldn't have lied about it. My guess is the gambling spot is not legal, and every dime you make is in cash, under the table. Am I right? Yeah, I'm right. You don't even have to answer. And I'm sorry, did you say you're a boss? Let me share a little secret with you: managing muthafuckas who can barely read and write or who get naked for dollar bills does not make you a boss! Don't try to cut in or check me about shit! You always talking about keeping stuff one hundred, well, let's keep one hundred. The truth of the matter is you started working for that low-life criminal who turned you on to the streets and was fucking you while you were a kid, because those are the types of people you like being around. You start working for a freakin' dope dealer who used to get your mom high, and now you want to act like this is a lucrative situation you're in. Girl, bye!"

Nina's feelings were beyond crushed. Rene had never talked down to her the way she was. "Fuck you, Rene. Fuck you for bringing that shit up. That was cold, regardless of how mad you are. Some lines you just don't cross," Nina managed to get out before going into her room.

The two women sat separately in their own rooms, not saying one word to one another. Rene was pretty sure steam was coming off the top of her head. She tried to play Bubble Pop! on her phone to occupy her thoughts. Just as she was running low on patience, the outside garage door came up. That was the sound Rene had been waiting for.

Rene jumped up and ran to Nina's room. She grabbed her by the arm and practically dragged her down the steps with her. She was moving so fast, Nina had to skip three steps just to keep from falling.

Jalen saw Rene and Nina rushing down the steps toward him and grew concerned. Everything was happening so fast, Jalen just stood there clueless, like his feet were planted in cement.

"Hey, baby. I'm so happy you're home. Please, have a seat, honey!" Rene said, grabbing Jalen's hand and leading both him and Nina into the living room. "Let's sit down and have a family chat! This is what you wanted to do, right?"

Although he was caught off guard, Jalen did not back down. "Yep! This is exactly what I wanted. I don't have a problem with that. Let's sit. Let's chat!"

Once the three of them were settled in the living room, the intense conversation instantly began. Rene knew this conversation was going to be loud and full of a lot of back and forth.

"How you gon' tell Rene that bullshit about me, Jalen? You know that's not the way shit flowed that night! Why are you making shit up?" screamed Nina.

"What?" said Jalen. "You sound stupid! That's exactly how it went down. You think your memory is so perfect and you remember different? Cool! Then let's hear it."

Nina began to explain. "I was drunk. That part is true. I didn't realize how drunk I was until we got to the hookah place. I never said those things about Rene. That I know for sure! I was dancing on Jalen, and he pushed me down. It wasn't even that serious. I thought he was just joking and got carried away. He wasn't mad or anything like that. When he and the security guy helped me up, Jalen was apologizing and everything. He never once yelled or cursed at me. Not once! When we got on the bus, I did not put my hand on his thigh on purpose. I was falling. I put my hand down to catch my balance. That was it! The nasty shit he said Shanequa was doing, that part was true. His friends paid her to do it. She was giving head in the back of the party bus, but I never, not once, offered it to Jalen. The thought of that shit makes me gag. If there is something inappropriate that I'm guilty of, it's dancing on Jalen in the bar and on the bus, rubbing his head while we were on the bus, and putting my breasts in his face when I was dancing on him. While I was dancing, he slipped a twenty-dollar bill in my cleavage for a tip, and I kissed him on his cheek. That was it! He made all that other shit up!" Nina promised.

"Not once did I say anything bad about you, Rene," Nina continued to defend herself. "Not once did I try to put my lips on his lips. I definitely did not try to grab his little-ass dick! Ugh! There is nothing I find attractive about this nigga. Drunk, sober, or high, I would never do that shit. He is wack as hell to me and always has been!" Nina wailed.

Jalen stood up, pissed off to the max. "You raggedy ho! I never put money in your cleavage! I was trying my best to get you away from me. Why would I do some dumb shit like that?" Jalen screamed at Nina.

Nina countered by sticking up both of her middle fingers and telling Jalen to kiss her ass.

Nina's antics infuriated Jalen. "Bitch, get out of my house! How you gonna sit there and tell these lies to my wife and then try to play me at the same time with your dumb-ass insults! I am so sick of you and your shit!"

Nina and Jalen began yelling back and forth, making Rene more and more upset. All of the yelling was giving Rene a headache. It was like someone had turned the volume up on a bad song and it was blaring in her ears. Rene finally couldn't take all the finger-pointing anymore and jumped up to shut it down.

"Shut the fuck up right now!" Rene yelled. "Both of you are getting on my damn nerves. The bottom line is both of y'all ain't shit! I don't care how you wanna slice this shit up. You both were dead-ass wrong. I can't trust either of you! You both betrayed me. Right now, I could beat the shit out of both of you! Quite frankly I'm disgusted at the sight of your faces. Jalen, you held this information in you for a year! Nina, if Jalen had not spilled the beans, you probably would have never told me. I can't live like this. Jalen, I think you should go. Nina, you got two weeks to get a place of your own, and I do mean two weeks."

"But, Rene," Nina pleaded, "you know I can't afford a place of my own."

"Sounds like you may have an issue on your hands, huh?" Rene answered coldly. "I'm sure your drug-dealing pedophile ex-boo will help you."

"Bae! I'm not going anywhere! This is just as much my house as it is yours!" Jalen said while turning Rene to face him.

Rene turned around and looked at Jalen. "You know what? You're absolutely right," replied Rene. "Give me a week. The kids and I will be out of here."

"Wait! That's not what I meant or want. Baby, no! Please, please, don't go. Wait a minute, Rene! Just wait!" Jalen said as Rene began to storm up the stairs.

Nina and Jalen began pleading and begging for Rene's forgiveness at the same time. Rene just wanted them to shut up.

"I said what I said! That's that! Leave me alone!" Rene screamed as she scolded the two. "Don't talk to me. Don't text me. Don't contact me on Facebook or Instagram. Leave me alone! Don't call me, I'll call you." Rene disappeared upstairs.

Nina just collapsed to the living room floor. She couldn't believe what had just transpired. She sat there lost in her thoughts. She felt as though someone was holding a pillow over her face, and she couldn't breathe.

Nina was drowning and drowning fast. Fear and frustration began to fill her mind and heart. Her friendship with Rene was always the solid constant in Nina's life, and she could feel that it was quickly slipping away from her. She couldn't imagine her life without their relationship, and it was something that she had no plans to ever experience. Rene and her family gave her love and loyalty that she'd never had before. There was no telling what might happen if she lost them.

"God, what is happening? Oh, my God! No, no, no, no! Please, don't leave me, Rene!" Nina cried. Nina's face became pale, and her eyes had no life in them. Her body went limp, her lips were trembling, and it appeared as if Nina had mentally blacked out.

"I gotta fix this! I gotta fix this! I can't lose her," Nina mumbled to herself. "I gotta fix this!"

Chapter 6

The Lunch Date

A couple of days had gone by since the big argument. After a long talk filled with screaming, cussing, and tears, Jalen finally accepted that it would be best if he left the house. He didn't want the kids to be affected by this stupid drama. He moved in with his cousin and would get the kids when he could.

Although he called Rene every day, several times a day, she refused to take his calls or even talk to him. She wouldn't even respond to his text messages unless it pertained to the kids. Her silent treatment was like none other. As brutal as it was, it did not make Jalen give up on his efforts. He had every intention of getting his family back. Whatever it took, he was going to do it.

Nina was still at the house. She and Rene did not talk at all. Nina would try to be cordial with Rene, ask her if she would like something to eat or if she could hold or watch the baby, anything to spark a conversation. Rene was not so willing to oblige. Rene still did all she could to assist with Jacob, but that was it. Nina knew that trying to regain Rene's trust and convince her that nothing more had happened was going to take a lot of work. She too was willing to do whatever was necessary to get her friend and friendship back.

Rene, on the other hand, was determined to get to the bottom of things. No matter what Jalen said, or what

Nina did, it did not make her believe that either of their versions was the whole truth or the end of the story. Rene knew in her heart and in her gut that something was not right. She wasn't going to rest until she had the whole story. She needed to know exactly what went down so that she would know how to properly punish them both.

One afternoon, while sitting in her office, Rene began to ponder her situation. She wished she had an inside man, someone who would not take sides, was reliable, and would have no problem exposing the truth regardless of who would end up looking bad.

Who could she call? Who could she trust? Who would know the extent of the situation and exactly what had happened? She couldn't call Jalen's cousin or his boys. They definitely would snitch on her or not be 100 percent honest. Most of them were idiots anyway. She wasn't cool with that ghetto, nasty-ass slut bucket Shanequa. That definitely wasn't an option. Even if she did call her, Shanequa would probably try to blackmail Rene. She even considered reaching out to Jody and DJ. Rene wasn't sure if they were there that night, but if there was a story to tell, she was certain that Shanequa told it to those two. After giving it a little more thought, she decided that Jody was too loyal and DJ was too fragile. They wouldn't be of any help to her.

Rene started thinking out loud. "Maybe this is something I will never know. Maybe I have to make a decision about the rest of my life based on the bullshit that Jalen and Nina have been feeding me," she said with a mixture of fear and disappointment in her voice.

As the day went on, Rene's mind continued to struggle with what was going on in her life. "Who's the one person who has a tie to all three of us and could possibly have some insight into all angles of the situation? Tyrese, that's who!" Rene said with excitement. Every time his name was brought up, both Jalen and Nina acted more nervous than a hooker in church. "Tyrese!" Rene thought out loud again. "Why didn't I think of him before?"

After the way she treated him the night she saw him in the pub and totally disregarded any of his efforts to fill her in, she doubted if he would even talk to her. Would he be willing to share something as deep and important as what Rene felt like Jalen and Nina were trying to hide?

"Hell, at this point, I'll try anything!" Rene said to herself. She flipped through her business cards and found Tyrese's number. As she dialed the number, she prayed that he would accept her call and be willing to talk to her.

"Tyrese Smalls and Associates, this is Maria. How may I help you?" said a squeaky voice on the other end.

"Hi, Maria, this is Rene Martin, a friend of Mr. Smalls'. Is he available to talk by chance?"

"Let me check on that for you!" said the receptionist.

She put Rene on hold, and seconds later Rene heard a sexy and familiar voice.

"This is Tyrese Smalls."

"Ummm, hey, Tyrese!" Rene nervously responded.

"Hello?" Tyrese repeated, not hearing Rene's initial response.

"Hey, it's . . . it's Rene." Rene began to stutter. "How are you?"

"Oh. Really?" said Tyrese. "Isn't this a pleasant surprise? Wow! To what do I owe the pleasure of this phone call?"

"Let's just say something really important has happened, and I need more details about what you were telling me regarding Nina and our friendship. I hope you can recall that conversation. Is there any way we can meet?" asked Rene.

Tyrese got the biggest grin on his face. Although he was more than willing to help Rene, he also had other things going through his mind and definitely a few tricks up his sleeve. "Yes, of course I remember. I'd be more than happy to meet with you. I can tell you anything you want to know. To be totally honest with you, I am surprised this phone call did not happen sooner. Either way, it would be nice just to see your beautiful face again," answered Tyrese.

Rene's stomach began to twist in a knot and hurt like she had eaten something bad. "All right, Tyrese, listen and listen good. I need your help. I need to know whatever it is that you know, and I am grateful for whatever you can provide. Let me correct that: I am beyond grateful. However, please keep in mind that I am still married, and I will not be disrespected, not by you or anyone else. Although I appreciate your compliments, they're truly inappropriate, and I'd rather you stop. This situation is uncomfortable enough. Please don't make it worse," Rene politely but firmly asked of Tyrese.

"Okay, Mrs. Rene!" Tyrese said. "I didn't realize I was coming on so strong. I didn't mean to ruffle any feathers or disrespect you. That was not my intention and never will be. I find you very attractive, and I guess I just got beside myself. Please accept my apology. I'm free for lunch for the remainder of the week. How about you?"

Rene looked through her calendar on her computer. She wanted to meet with Tyrese, and she knew that this lunch get-together would not be a quick in-and-out meeting. Depending on what he told her, she might not be able to return to work. She also had to take into consideration that she did not want their encounter to get back to Jalen or Nina. Until she figured out what her game plan was, she did not want them to know that she and Tyrese had met.

"How about you meet me at the pizzeria off old 64?" Rene suggested.

"You mean the one that's back off the dirt road? If I recall correctly, it looks like an old house," Tyrese said.

"Yes, that's one. Is that a problem? Can you meet me there?" Rene asked.

Tyrese snickered. "Yeah, I guess. Will it be safe? I mean, you're not going to have a hit man or a sniper waiting on the roof for me, are you?"

Rene couldn't help but laugh. "No, I am not cut like that. Besides, I need you way too much to have you knocked off. Maybe afterward," she cleverly replied.

Rene and Tyrese agreed on a time to meet the next day and ended their phone conversation. Rene finished the portfolio she was working on and let her assistant know that she was going to being leaving a little early.

At home, it was so hard for Rene to concentrate and behave like she normally would. The anticipation of meeting Tyrese the next day had completely invaded her thoughts.

Oh, my God! What is this man about to tell me? Do I really want to know what he has to say? Am I ready for this? Maybe I should call and cancel. Maybe I should just forget the whole thing. I mean, what if he says something that will totally devastate me? They both were drunk. Technically, nothing really happened. They both have apologized. Just let it go, Rene, just let it go. Rene tried to convince herself that everything was okay, but it wasn't working.

Was it worth enduring the heartache and the pain that this meeting may bring her to possibly be worse off than what she already was? There was something about the situation that would not allow her to let it go. She could not just forgive Jalen and Nina and put it all behind her, partially because it was too fresh, and partially because she didn't feel like she had the entire truth. The last thing she wanted was to forgive them, move on with life, then find out later there was more to the story and have to emotionally start all over again.

"You know what? I'm going to meet with Tyrese, and I'll make my decision from there," she said, still trying to believe that she was making the right decision. Rene finally was able to let her mind slow down and release all of the back-and-forth energy she had accumulated throughout the day. After tossing and turning for hours, she drifted off to sleep.

When her alarm clock went off, Rene shot straight up like a kid on Christmas Day. That excitement quickly went away, and she fell straight back and tried to disappear into her pile of pillows. This was the moment of truth, the moment she had been waiting for. The kids were now visiting with Jalen's parents, and she only had two days left before they would be returning home. Any moves she was going to make had to be made before they came back. It would be too hard to explain if they were there.

She quickly took a shower, got herself together, and headed out the door. She had a few errands to run before she met with Tyrese: go grocery shopping, get an oil change, and take some bills to the post office. As she walked downstairs, she heard Jacob crying.

Ugh. Where is his trifling mama?

She went upstairs to find Nina in the shower singing an old TLC song, with Jacob in his crib screaming. She walked into Nina's room to get Jacob and try to comfort him.

"What's wrong, big man?" Rene said as she picked him up and held him close. "Calm down, it's okay! Don't cry!" She fixed Jacob a bottle, changed his diaper, and laid him back in his crib.

"Hey!" Rene yelled, banging on the bathroom door.

Nina jumped from the loud bang. "Yyyyeeah, what's up?"

"I'm leaving. The baby has a bottle. Don't stay in the shower too long. He was crying, and you couldn't hear him," Rene informed her.

"Oh, my bad, thank you!" Nina bellowed back to Rene.

Nina waited for Rene's response, but it never came. Rene was out the door, in her car, and on her way to handle her business before her lunch meeting with Tyrese.

Rene got to the pizzeria a little early. She went in and got them a table. As she sat there, she started shaking her legs, becoming more and more anxious for this meeting to get started.

When Tyrese pulled up in his black Mercedes-Benz, she found herself examining him from head to toe, and she instantly started to admire him. There was no denying that Tyrese was a fine-looking milk-chocolate brotha. He just had the type of face and body that made her want to kiss him all over.

"What are you doing?" Rene whispered, starting to chastise herself. "You're just as big a slut as Nina is." She got herself together, cleared her mind, and greeted Tyrese as he walked through the door.

"Good day, gorgeous!" Tyrese said.

Rene managed to put half a smile on her face. "What did we talk about, sir? How about, 'Hello, Rene'?" she reminded him.

Tyrese let out a little chuckle. "Yes. I remember. You are right. I'll try harder." Tyrese's chuckle turned into a full laugh. "Girl, you are something else, and you're fine as hell, too."

Rene cracked a smile even though she really didn't want to. "Look here, man! We are here on business. I told you that! Now cut it out, and stop playing so much," Rene firmly said to Tyrese.

"Yes, ma'am. Business only, ma'am!" Tyrese joked while giving Rene a military salute. "Can I at least get a business hug seeing that I am doing you this big favor and all?"

Rene let out a sigh. She went ahead and gave Tyrese a hug. He smelled sooo good. His arms wrapped around her waist like a security blanket. She couldn't help but lay her head on his chest. Rene snapped out of her daze and quickly pulled away. "All right, that's enough of that. Please sit down. The pizza is on me," she said.

"Okay, cool. I appreciate that. I am quite hungry," said Tyrese sarcastically.

The two began to talk. Tyrese was full of small-talk type of questions. How were the kids? How was work? Did she like her coworkers? Blah, blah, blah. Rene had no interest in catching up on old times or what was going on in each other's lives.

Finally, Rene couldn't take it anymore. "Enough with the small talk or whatever. I'm not trying to rude, but that is not why we are here," Rene said, interrupting Tyrese midsentence. "I am not trying to be your friend. I need you to tell me what's going on. What is it that you know about Nina? What makes her such a horrible person?"

Tyrese wiped his mouth with his napkin. He looked into Rene's eyes. They said it all. There was no denying that she was emotionally distraught.

"Understood." Tyrese began, "Are you sure you ready for this, Rene? This shit is not some fairy tale, and I can guarantee you there is a huge chance that there will not be a happy ending."

Rene looked away, hanging her head and staring at the pizza on her plate in front of her. She could tell by the look on his face and the sincerity in his eyes that what he was about to tell her was nothing good.

She thought about it briefly. *Do I really want to know this?* Her answer to herself was, *no, I need to know this.* She grabbed Tyrese's hand and said, "Yes! Please tell me. I need to know. I'm ready."

"Okay then. There it is. What I'm about to tell you is not something that I'm proud of. Let me get that off my chest first," Tyrese began to explain to Rene. "However, I want you to know that it's the one hundred percent total truth, and I'll say this in front of Nina, Jalen, and whomever else I need to," he assured Rene.

Rene gave Tyrese a nod of agreement, signaling to keep going.

"One day when I came home from work, I heard Nina on the phone. She was laughing and giggling and really into the conversation. However, it wasn't the normal laughing and giggle, ya know? It was the type of laugh and giggle she used to do with me. I was thrown off. She was so into it she didn't even hear me come in. I sat and I listened. She said how much she missed this person on the phone and how happy they made her feel. She then said she would be glad when they could see each other again. When she wrapped up her conversation and got off the phone, I didn't confront her. Me being who I am, I needed all my ducks in a row before I went any further. Instead of blowing up and getting upset over a bunch of assumptions, I decided to follow her and collect evidence of whatever she was doing myself."

Rene's palms were starting to sweat. The longer Tyrese talked, the more fear and anxiety built up inside of her. The anticipation was killing Rene.

Tyrese continued, “One night, she told me she had to work. I knew she was lying because earlier in the week she had already told me she had this particular night off. I could have reminded her about our previous conversation, but I didn’t. I decided that this was the night I would follow her. I told her I had to drop some documents off to a client. I switched cars with a friend of mine and waited at the end of my block for her to leave. I started following her, and I couldn’t believe where she was going. Now mind you, at this time she was like eight months pregnant with what I thought was my baby. I’m thinking, *where in the world is she going at this time of night with my baby inside of her?* When I got to the destination, I was speechless. I couldn’t believe she was doing this to me.”

“Doing what to you?” Rene said.

“She was at a hotel,” answered Tyrese.

“At a hotel?” Rene’s stomach slumped. “At a hotel for what?”

“Let me finish,” Tyrese requested. “After she went in, I went up to the desk and asked if she was registered. She wasn’t. I went back to the car. As I’m sitting in the parking lot waiting, trying to figure out what’s going on and what my next move was, I spot a familiar vehicle. A vehicle that I had seen before when I was with Nina, dropping her off at your house. It was Jalen’s truck.”

Rene’s tears were beginning to form. *I can’t let him see me cry! Suck it up! This is what you wanted, and now you’re getting it! There is no turning back now.*

“I went back inside,” Tyrese continued, “back to the desk, and I asked if there was a Jalen Martin registered. The clerk said yes and offered to call up to his room. I said no and left. My blood was boiling over! I got a copy of Nina’s cell phone records to get a look into what was going on. She and Jalen talked every day, sometimes multiple times a day. I started thinking, *why is she meeting her best friend's husband at a hotel, and why is she on the phone with her best friend's husband for so much? What in the hell are they talking about? What are they up to?*"

"What happened after that?" Rene asked.

"I still didn't confront her," Tyrese replied. "I couldn't. I didn't have enough evidence to make a solid case. There were still too many holes she could have used to maneuver out of it or create a cover story."

"Are you kidding me?" Rene asked, clearly bothered by what she'd heard. "They met at the freakin' hotel! What type of story could she come up with that could explain that?"

"I didn't see Jalen go in with her, and I didn't actually see him at the hotel. I only saw his truck. She could have easily said that it was you she was with. She could have easily said that she was helping Jalen throw a surprise party for you, and that's why they were talking on the phone so much. She could have easily said a bunch of things, and there would have been no way for me to prove her wrong," Tyrese explained to Rene.

"Dang, you right! I never thought of that!"

"Well, I did!" said Tyrese. "So, I kept it to myself, and I grinned and bore it as long as I could. Finally, I got what I needed."

"Did you follow her again?" inquired Rene.

"I hired a private investigator."

"A private investigator? Oh goodness! This shit is like a real-life soap opera!" Rene said in disbelief.

Tyrese nodded in agreement. "Welcome to your world, baby. Welcome to your world!"

Those words hit Rene like a ton of bricks. "Welcome to my world! What in the Lord's name have I gotten myself into?" Rene said, shaking her head. "Okay, just finish."

Tyrese did as he was told. "I hired the private investigator, and after about two or three weeks of following her and doing what he had to do, he called me and told me that he needed to meet with me. He said his investigation was over and he had something for me. When I met with him, deep down inside I was praying and hoping that he was going to say I had nothing to worry about. She was just helping her friend's husband plan something for her friend, and that's all it was. You know, something like that. Anything but what I heard. Rene, it's about to get ugly. What I'm about to say is going to hurt. I have to warn you."

Rene could no longer play the tough role. Tears came down her face, and she could not stop them. "It's already ugly," she said softly.

Tyrese grabbed her hand. "That's all right. I got your back. Whatever you need me to do, I will do for you. I'm going to help you through this!"

Rene once again motioned Tyrese to continue with the story.

"I get to the meeting spot. The investigator pulled out an envelope. In this envelope were pictures. Pictures of Jalen and Nina, arm in arm, talking in parking lots, eating at a restaurant, and even coming out of a few hangout spots. There was a picture of them hugging, and another of Nina kissing him on the cheek. The investigator went on to tell me that they didn't meet every day. However, when they did connect, they would be together for hours. He also said he attempted to follow them into a couple of the spots they went to, but he was denied entry. They were invitation-only places. I left him and headed home. My mind was racing. My heart was shattered into a million pieces. I was a total mess! I take all of the info and the photo that he gave me and put them on our kitchen table. When Nina got home and saw everything, she just stood there looking at me with this dumb look on her face. I ask her what the hell is going on! Do you know what she said to me?" Tyrese asked in a bold whisper.

"What?" Rene responded in a faint voice.

"She tells me that she is so sorry for lying to me and that she never meant to hurt me. However, she was somewhat relieved that I found out. She was tired of living a double life. I asked her what it all meant. Her response was that she's in love with Jalen, Jalen is in love with her, and she's not pregnant by me. She's pregnant by him."

Rene felt dizzy, like there was a plastic bag over her head. It was becoming harder and harder for her to breathe. She felt as if she could have just passed out right there on the floor of the pizzeria. Her worst fears were now her truth, and she was struggling to take it all in.

"Oh, my God!" Rene yelled. "Oh, my God! Why? Why me?" she yelled even louder.

People in the restaurant were starting to look at them. Tyrese didn't want people to become concerned or try to get involved thinking they were intervening in some domestic situation gone bad. "Come on," he said. "Let's go outside."

He dropped $25 on the table for the check. He grabbed Rene's hand, helped her out of her chair, and walked outside. Rene was so weak her knees started to buckle, and it was hard for her to stand straight up. She could not believe what Tyrese had just told her.

"You're lying!" she cried. "You have got to be lying. You're just saying this to make me mad. You're just saying this to get back at Nina. Please, Tyrese. Please tell me you are lying."

Tyrese held Rene close to him. "I wish I were. I promise on everything that I love, I wish I were lying about all of this shit. You don't deserve this. Hell, I don't deserve this.

Doesn't change the fact that it's the truth. I was thinking she had something going on with that chick Jody. They were all of sudden doing everything together and were the best of friends. We both know that Nina has a freaky side to her. The joke was on me though. The whole time it was really Jalen. That's why I put Nina out. That's why I threw all of her stuff outside. That's why I took her phone and took her car. I would never in a million years abandon my child, regardless of whether I was still with the mother. But why would I take care of another man's woman and baby? I'm a good guy, but I'm nobody's fool. I didn't care how much I loved her and wanted to be with her. Her ass had to go."

"Why didn't you say something to me before now? I moved this bitch into my house!" said Rene, puzzled.

"I mean, I really wasn't close to you like that," said Tyrese. "After I put Nina out, I wasn't talking to her or trying to keep tabs on her at all. And honestly, she was our only connection, so I just—"

"But you didn't say anything the other night when I saw you either," Rene interrupted. "Why didn't you tell me then? I've had her in my house all this time, and she's been screwing my husband. I let her take care of my kids! Hell, I've left them there alone. Who knows what they've been doing right up under my nose?"

"All I can say is now you know, so get a good attorney, because you're going to need one. I have copies of everything that I can get to you if you need it. I'm willing to help you in any way I can with anything. I do mean anything! This is not going to be easy for you. I know a lot of people, and I have a ton of resources. I'm your guy," Tyrese offered.

"You're my who, sir?" Rene curiously asked.

"I meant that like I'm your friend! Your go-to guy. The plug! You know what I mean!" Tyrese said with a smirk on his face. He then took his thumb and wiped away the tears on Rene's cheek.

Rene shook her head and pulled away. "Look, Tyrese, I'm going to be honest with you. I find you attractive. Shit, I think you're fine as hell, and yeah, you are fly as fuck, too. Your swagger is to die for! There is no denying that. I'm just not cut like that. Maybe . . . who knows, twenty or thirty years from now, if I'm not in jail for killing Jalen and Nina, we can go on a real date. As of right now, all you are doing is adding to the level of annoyance that's inside of me."

Tyrese backed up. "I wasn't trying to come on to you. I was just trying to help lighten the air a little. I didn't mean to offend you, but I meant what I said. If there is anything you ever need from me, you let me know!"

Rene paused, looked down at the ground, and took a deep breath. She slowly lifted her head. "Thank you, Tyrese. I appreciate the offer. I appreciate you."

"No problem!" Tyrese answered.

"I do have one last question for you. I hope that's okay."

"Anything. Ask away."

"You said you have a lot of resources. Well, do you know where I can buy a gun? I think I might need one."

Tyrese stood there with his mouth open, stunned and speechless.

Chapter 7

Can You Say Revenge?

As Rene pulled out of the parking lot, tears were running down her face so hard and fast it was like a rainstorm was streaming out of her eyes. She could barely see the road ahead of her. The rage that was fighting to jump out of her chest was a feeling she had never experienced before. She could not wrap her mind around the things that had just been shared with her.

Her husband and her best friend, the two people she loved the most, the two people she trusted the most had committed the ultimate betrayal. To put the icing on the cake, the baby boy she loved so much and treated as her own could possibly be her stepson.

"What the hell!" Rene screamed, banging her hands on the steering wheel. She had never felt so many different emotions at one time.

Her first thought was to kill them both. She thought she would take Nina out first.

"Maybe I can wait for her to go to school. After she drops the baby off, I can just follow her, run her off the road, and be done with it!" Rene contemplated to herself. "But what if she doesn't die? No, that won't work. I know! I can pretend to go out of town, wait until it's late, and then break in the house. Kill them both at one time. Save myself the trouble of trying to come up with two plans. I can do the job myself. No, wait, then Jacob will be there by himself until someone finds them. Uggghhhh!" Rene yelled as she pounded her fist on the steering wheel.

As Rene continued to brainstorm different plans to kill Nina and Jalen, it clicked in her head that by doing so, she would leave three innocent children without a mother and a father, especially if she got caught. She could not put her children through such pain because of her own anger and self-gain.

However, they had to pay, and they had to pay big. Rene paused her thoughts of revenge for a moment to figure out where she was going to go. She couldn't go home. That would be nothing short of a massacre by the time she finished with Nina's skank ass. She couldn't go to her mother's. She was out of town visiting her family in the South, and Rene did not have the keys to her house with her. After driving aimlessly for over an hour, she decided to just get a hotel room and sort out her thoughts.

After all the years she had invested in her marriage, how could Jalen do this to her? She knew that men cheated on their wives, but she never thought Jalen would. He was so dedicated to his family. He never gave her a reason not to trust him. After she considered all the things that had transpired over the last year, it began to make sense.

Nina always seemed to think Jalen was up to no good. She pointed out when he was an hour late getting home, on the phone longer than usual, or behaving strangely. Things that Rene never seemed to notice or think were issues, Nina did. Sometimes she would get so angry that Rene would have to calm her down and tell her to relax. Nina wasn't getting angry because she thought Jalen was doing Rene dirty. Nina was getting so angry because she felt as though Jalen was doing her dirty!

Whenever Jalen wanted to hang out with his friends, maybe go for a drink after work, Rene wouldn't care at all. In fact, Rene encouraged Jalen to do things on his own, without her and the kids. Although her parents were no longer together, Rene's mom would tell her often that a man needed his space. He needed time away from reality to regroup and recharge. Rene believed that everyone needs a little R&R every now and then. Nina on the other hand would be so irritated. Sometimes she would be livid! She needed to know the when, the who, and the where of Jalen's every move. If she asked Rene a question about Jalen and Rene didn't know, Nina would flip out and tell Rene she was dumb for not demanding that Jalen share every detail with her. That wasn't to benefit Rene. It was to benefit Nina.

Nina would try her best to get Rene to feel the same way she did. Rene never did. It just wasn't that important to her, and she trusted Jalen. If Jalen was going to play a pickup game or go to the local sports bar to watch football on the big screen, Nina would have a fit if he didn't take Rene or the kids with him.

"Why can't he take you?" Nina would ask. "I mean hell, you like sports too." Rene would shrug it off and chalk it up to Nina just being overprotective.

When Jalen was at home, if he was a little clingy with Rene or if Rene did things like make his plate or iron his clothes, Nina would turn into a full-blown women's rights activist. She would give Rene long rants on how Jalen was trying to control her, how this wasn't the 1960s, and she no longer had to be barefoot, pregnant, and in the kitchen, catering to her man. Rene chalked that up to maybe Nina being a little bitter about her situation with Tyrese, so she just brushed it off. Looking back on things, Rene realized that Nina was jealous. She didn't like Jalen being affectionate with Rene. Nina wanted to be the one doing acts of love for Jalen. That's where all her frustration was coming from.

Now that all the secrets had been unveiled and the truth was out, everything had a different meaning. Everything was totally different from what it had seemed. Everything Rene had believed was a lie!

Rene starting having flashbacks. The numerous times that Nina couldn't get the answers she wanted or couldn't get Rene to be as curious as she was, her anger would be on another level! She would even go so far as to say little smart comments belittling Rene, like, "If you want to be stupid, then be stupid," and, "If he were my husband, he wouldn't be running the streets at night with his single friends."

I get it now. She was so worked up all the time because she thought she was his woman. She wasn't concerned about him cheating on me. She was concerned about him cheating on her! That low-down, dirty-ass, triflin' bitch!

Rene pulled into the parking lot of the Courtyard Marriot. She was a rewards member there and knew she could use her points so that the room purchase wouldn't show up on any bank statements. She and Jalen were still sharing a joint bank account.

Once she was settled in her room, Rene became very anxious. She started to pace the floor and pound her fist into her hand. Her blood was pumping so fast and hard through her veins it caused her head to throb from an intense headache, and her nose began to bleed. She didn't even realize it until she glanced in the mirror and saw red stains on her sweatshirt. She went to the bathroom and cleaned off her face. No matter what she did, the blood would not stop coming. She got a cold towel and lay back on the bed. She tried her best to calm herself down, but it wasn't working. Her towel quickly filled up with the bright red fluid, causing her to go back to the bathroom to rinse it out and try again.

"You have to calm down!" Rene pleaded with herself. "You cannot let this break you."

She lay back down to try to relax, once again being unsuccessful. Every time she closed her eyes, she kept having visions of Jalen and Nina together. Visions of them holding hands, laughing, kissing, and having sex consumed her brain.

Jalen was so against Nina moving in. All of a sudden, he went from "she's cool, I don't have a problem with her" to hating her guts and never wanting her to be around. Why? Rene couldn't figure it out.

If Nina was his lover, and Jacob was his baby, why did he behave the way he did? You would think he would want them around. Maybe it was just too close for comfort for him. Maybe he thought that by Nina and the baby living with them, Rene would find out the truth.

What really began to piss Rene off was that Jalen let it all happen. Yes, Nina was her friend, but Jalen was her husband. They made a vow to each other and to God to always take care of each other and be there for one another. Not only had he been having an affair, but it was with her best friend. Her best friend who he knew lived a very carefree and risky life. She was wild, and it was not a secret. Jalen had unprotected sex with a woman of this nature and produced a child. He could have brought home a disease to Rene, and he didn't seem to care. If he did care, he wouldn't have done it.

What if Tyrese was cheating on Nina while this affair was going on? What if Nina had another guy on the side in addition to Tyrese and Jalen? Nina could have gotten an STD from Tyrese or someone else, passed it to Jalen, and then given it to Rene. The thought of all the potential passing from person to person made Rene nauseated. Did Jalen even love her anymore? He couldn't have. If he did, he would not have put her at risk the way he did.

Nothing will cause a person to question his or her worth like a betrayal. Rene started to question her role in all of this, as she imagined many women in her position would. Did she stop being the wife he wanted and needed? Did she push him into Nina's arms by being so dedicated to her work? Was it her own selfish needs that made her push so hard to have Nina live with them and help out with the kids and housework?

"Shake this shit off, Rene! This is not your fault!" Rene shouted, trying to offer herself some encouragement. "No matter what the problem was, he could have come to me. He could have just left me. He could have done anything other than what he did! This shit is not my fault!"

Rene began to cry uncontrollably. A few times she had to jump from the bed and run into the bathroom to vomit. Her head was pounding, her stomach ached, and from her head to her toes, her entire body was going numb. She was shaking, and her mind was racing with images and thoughts that seemed to be controlling her very being. After a few hours had passed, her body gave in and shut down. Rene cried herself to sleep.

When Rene woke up, for whatever reason her mind was much clearer. She sat up in the oversized bed and stretched her arms. She took a hot shower to relax her extremely tense body.

"Wow. I'm starving!" Rene said as she picked up the menu for the restaurant that was connected to the hotel. She ordered herself something to eat and turned on the television. As she flipped through the channels, she discovered that her favorite movie of all time, *The Five Heartbeats,* was on.

She slipped into the oversized shirt she had purchased from Target before she got to the hotel. She curled up under the covers and waited for her food to arrive. After about thirty minutes, there was a knock at the door.

"Who is it?" Rene yelled.

"Sharky's Bistro! I have your food order."

Rene got out of bed, grabbed $20 out of her wallet, and walked over to the door. She looked through the peephole. A short Hispanic young man, a little on the heavy side, held a delivery bag. He wore a black fitted cap with a shark dressed like a chef on the front of it. The same image was on the front of his T-shirt. She opened the door just enough to slide half of her body out to grab her food.

"Here you are," Rene said, handing the young man the money. "Keep the change."

"Thank you, ma'am. Enjoy your meal." The delivery guy handed Rene her food.

Rene closed the door and sat on the bed to eat her favorite type of salad, a Michigan Traverse City with grilled chicken, and to continue to watch her favorite movie. She was doing all she could to stay as relaxed as possible.

After the movie went off, she knew that it was time to come back and face reality. She got a pad and pen and sat at the small desk in the room. She began to make a list of the things she needed to take care of leading up to filing for divorce from Jalen.

Pre-divorce list:
1. Secure the bag and home

The townhouse, cars, and bank accounts were all in her name, so he would get what she chose for him to have. She made more money than Jalen, so she thought that alimony might be an issue.

"That's okay. I'll pay it. Especially if it means he will be out of my life," she said to herself.

2. My babies

Regardless of everything going on, Jalen was an incredible father. Rene could not deny that even if she wanted to. Earlier in their relationship, in the midst of a random conversation, Jalen boldly told Rene that no matter what happened between them, she would never take the kids from him. He said it with a straight face and serious eyes. He declared that he would fight her until there was no breath left in his body.

With that in mind, Rene knew she couldn't let her personal feelings get in the way of any custody agreements. She would have to stay fair and not put the kids through an ugly custody battle. She would have to be okay with joint custody. Rene loved her kids, and they were without a doubt the most important thing in her life. She didn't want to put them through any unnecessary drama. The separation would be hard enough.

3. Get proof

Even though she did not want to, she was going to have to contact Tyrese and ask for copies of the photos he had. She was going to take a page from his book and not confront Jalen without any evidence. With the pics in hand, Jalen wouldn't be able to deny anything.

4. Revenge!

Rene had always been a strategic type of woman. Unlike Nina, she made sure that everything she did was well planned out. She had a system she operated under:

assess, brainstorm, confirm a plan of action, and execute. In her mind, this revenge plot wasn't any different. Now it was time to solidify her plan.

Her course of action had to be a surprise attack. It had to hit hard and quick. Initially the ultimate revenge seemed obvious: get with Tyrese.

As Rene thought back to her meeting with Tyrese, she couldn't help but think about how scrumptious he looked. He was the definition of fine. Tyrese was every woman's fantasy. His physical appearance was clearly designed by God Himself.

He was also charming, had undeniable swag and sex appeal, was hung like a horse, and knew exactly what to do with it! Rene could just imagine the feeling of his strong hands caressing her body and making her feel secure. She could almost feel the stiffness of his long, thick manhood filling her body with uncontrollable delight while she yearned for him to give her more. The scent of his cologne was still in her nose, and that was all she could seem to smell. It was almost like he was in the room with her. The way he held her when they embraced for a hug triggered something inside of her lady box. There wasn't any denying that.

Rene smiled. If she felt like that with a simple hug, imagine what it would be like to be embraced in a kiss, or to have his arms wrapped around her waist to gently lay her down so that they could enjoy each other intimately.

Before Rene knew it, her hand had found its way down the front of her black lace panties and onto her throbbing clit. She gently started to rub in a circular motion, pleasuring herself at the thought of Tyrese pleasing her. Within a few minutes, soft moans left her mouth at quick intervals. Soon she let out a loud sigh of erotic pleasure as she climaxed and her juices began to flow and soak her panties. As her self-inflicted high slowly came down,

Rene realized that even though her fantasy started out with a vision of Tyrese's face, it ended with visions of her and Jalen. This revelation lightweight pissed Rene off. Jalen didn't deserve to be a part of her pleasure.

It had been quite some time since Rene felt like she and Jalen were making love and not just satisfying a need they both had, that need being fulfilling their horniness. She had a feeling that if she were to go ahead and do the damn thang with Tyrese, he could give her the fire and passion she had been missing and yearning for. Putting herself in a situation to make that happen would be a piece of cake.

Tyrese had already let it be known that he was very much interested in her, so there was no convincing or seducing that Rene had to do. Who knew? Maybe hooking up could work out for both of them. Rene could use Tyrese to help her get through the chaos that had invaded her life, and Rene could help him quench the curiosity he had developed for her. *There is nothing like a great sex buddy to relieve some stress and help take your mind off the problems in your world.*

"Well, there you have it. I'll call Tyrese. Ask him to bring the pictures to the hotel. Once he is here, I will make sure that he can't resist me. It will be on and poppin'! I will put it on him so tough he'll forget his own name. It'll be a three-for-one special. I'll get my revenge on Nina and Jalen, get my rocks off, and get the evidence I need all at the same time," Rene proudly said to herself.

She was pleased with her master plan and grabbed her cell phone to call Tyrese. As she looked for his number to text him, Rene paused. She was doing the very thing her dad had taught her not to do.

"Never let people or a situation change who you are and what you stand for," Rene could hear her father saying in her head. Having random sex with a man for revenge was not her style at all. She was without a doubt

not that type of woman. Never in her life had she had casual sex with a man, and it would be flat-out dumb for her to start now. And who was to say that Tyrese meant everything he said? Maybe he wasn't serious about them being there for each other and him helping her any way he could. Nina said that Tyrese had his share of the ladies before they started dating. Since Nina hurt him so bad, maybe he was bitter and had a "hit it and quit it" plan of his own in the works, and then Rene would be nothing more than a casualty of war. To be used twice would be just too much to handle. So now she was back to square one.

Trying to figure out a great plan of revenge that would not put her children in harm's way or cause her to feel like a nasty whore in the morning, was going to be a lot tougher than Rene thought. She decided to just go with her gut. If she could just get Jalen and Nina together, she was confident that her creativity would kick in and she would be able to let them have it.

Jalen was no longer staying at the house, which caused a slight problem. She had to figure out a way to get them in the same room, without looking suspicious. Rene was going to have to play a role so good that she could be nominated for an Academy Award, and she was up for the challenge. The hurt and anger that flowed through her heart was giving her the courage to do things she wouldn't dare even think about under normal circumstances. Her pleasant and cautious demeanor was quickly going out the window. She was game to allow the evil side of her come out and release the wrath that was brewing inside of her.

Ring, ring!

"Hello?" said Jalen.

"Hey, it's me," said Rene.

"Hey, babe! I mean, Rene. What's up? Is everything okay?"

"Everything's fine. You busy? Do you have a minute to talk?"

Jalen was nervous, like he was talking to the popular girl at school he had a crush on. He quickly went from lying down to sitting straight up on the couch. Hearing Rene's voice sent a chill down his back. He missed her so much.

"I'm not busy at all," he said. "I'm just sitting here watching TV and snacking on some chips. What's on your mind? You sound like you've been crying."

Rene rolled her eyes. "No, I'm cool. I've just been doing some thinking, that's all. I need to ask you something."

"Okay. Go ahead."

"Are you telling me the whole story and truth about what went down with you and Nina? And before you answer me, I need you to truly think about this entire situation and what it is doing to us. If there is any hope for us to work this thing out, I need to know that you care more about being honest and my feelings than you do about whatever consequences may come from owning your shit."

There was a short spell of silence before Jalen answered her. The request threw Jalen for a loop, more than Rene calling did. For him, her asking him that meant that she still was questioning his honesty. He may have hidden things from Rene, but as far as he was concerned, he had never lied to her. This level of mistrust was new for her.

"Rene, you know that I love you and the kids with everything inside of me. I can admit when I am wrong, and that is exactly what I have done. I should have told you about that night as soon as I got home. If I had done that, then you would not have wanted Nina to move in with us, and we wouldn't be in this situation. Baby, I promise you,

I have told you everything. I did not touch her. I did not want to touch her. That night happened the way I said it happened. If Nina, or anyone else for that matter, tells you anything different, then they are lying to you."

"Jalen, I—"

"Wait, I'm not done. I know that is your friend, but trust me, she is a backstabbing ho. She is jealous of you and does not have your back the way she says she does. I'm so sorry for taking you on this roller coaster and not trusting that you would be able to make rational decisions. I love you. I just want to come home and for us to be a family again. I'll do whatever it takes. Whatever you want me to do to make this work. You are my everything, and I can't be without you."

Tears began to fall from Rene's eyes. As always, listening to Jalen plead his case was hitting a soft spot. Even though he still was lying about what happened with him and Nina, Rene knew that deep down inside he had learned his lesson. Even though so many negative thoughts and feelings were at the forefront of her mind, she did love her husband. Before that day, divorce was not something she was ever really ready to accept. He sounded so sincere.

Unfortunately for him, his sincerity had come a little too late.

It took her a minute to regain her composure and snap out of her trance. Rene cleared her throat and got back to the business at hand. "I love you too, Jalen. Maybe we should talk face-to-face. A conversation of this magnitude deserves to take place where we can see each other's eyes and feel the true emotion in what we are saying."

"Okay. Okay. That's cool. Umm, where do you wanna meet? Uh, you wanna come over to Donavan's? Or how about I treat you to some seafood at the Detroit Seafood Market? We can meet at that one spot on Livernois. You said you liked it there and that the wings were good. I mean, we can go where—"

"Jalen! Slow down! Don't make this weirder than it already is."

"My bad. You're right."

"Can you just come by the house in the morning around ten thirty? The kids are still with your parents, so we will have some privacy."

"Sure. I can do that. Anything you want, I will do. You said at about ten thirty, right?"

"Hmmm, better make it eleven thirty. I want to be able to sleep in and not have to rush to get dressed."

"Okay, cool. Eleven thirty it is. I guess I'll see you then."

"Yep. Goodbye."

When Rene hung up, her stomach began to get the nervous butterfly feeling. What if her plan didn't work? What if she wasn't able to control her emotions and ruined the entire thing? What would she do then? What if Tyrese was making this whole thing up as a way to hurt Nina's feelings? Could she really trust him? If he had pictures, why didn't he bring them with him to the first meeting?

Then again, everything he said matched up with other events and situations that had taken place. If Jalen knew that Nina had confessed the truth to Tyrese, it would really explain why they both almost wet themselves whenever Tyrese's name was mentioned or if he walked into a room.

Rene determined that the doubt she was having was just an emotional reaction to her behaving outside of her character. If it was more than her nerves, then she would just cross that bridge when she got to it. There was no time or reason to turn back now. After months of being lied to and treated like a naive fool, it was time to take her rightful position as queen bee and show them that no one, *no one,* took advantage of her.

She was too exhausted to do anything else. Rene got back into bed and looked for something to watch on TV. *I guess I'd better get my rest. I'm in for a long day tomorrow, and I will definitely need all of my strength and energy.* She adjusted the pillows and got comfortable.

After finding a channel that was having a *Golden Girls* marathon, Rene snuggled up under the cover and slowly allowed her mind to be at ease. Before long she was no longer watching TV, but instead it was watching her.

Chapter 8

Hell Yeah, It's On!

When Rene opened her eyes, she felt as though she had been riding an amusement park ride for hours. Everything seemed hazy and foggy. Her first thoughts were that she was still dreaming. This false sense of reality was quickly removed when her cell phone rang, and the caller ID said Husband.

"Shit!" mumbled Rene. "What the hell does he want?" She answered, "Yeah?"

"Good morning!" said Jalen. "Did I wake you?"

"Yes. I mean, no. Kind of. I'm somewhat awake. I'm just lying here."

"Oh, okay. I wanted to make sure we are still on for this morning."

"Yep. Why? What time is it?"

"It's eight forty-six. Okay, great. I'll see you in a little bit. Would you like me to bring breakfast? I can stop and grab you one of those omelets you love from IHOP."

"Considering that I clearly said I wanted to sleep in and you still called me early as hell, no, thank you. I'm fine. All I want is another thirty minutes to relax before I get up."

"Aww shit! You did say that, didn't you? My bad, babe. I totally forgot. Okay, talk to you later."

Rene rolled over and put her phone on the charger. She lay in bed and daydreamed a little longer before finally heading to the bathroom. She washed her face, brushed her teeth, and combed her hair. She slipped into her clothes and looked at herself in the mirror.

"Okay, girl. This is it. The moment of truth. No matter what either of them says, stick to your guns and hold your ground. This is your show! You run this! When it's all said and done, you will have the last laugh. Be you. Love you. Do you." Rene's self-encouragement via her pep talk gave her an energy boost! Her adrenaline was on ten, and she could barely keep still.

She packed up all of her things, grabbed her phone, and texted Tyrese. She figured texting was the safer route just in case he wasn't alone.

Rene: Hello, Tyrese. This is Rene. Sorry for the short notice, but do you think you can meet me at the Lowe's on Ford Rd. in Dearborn in about 30 minutes? I would like to get those pictures if that's okay.

Tyrese: Good morning. No problem at all. I just finished my morning run, so good timing.

Rene: That is perfect! Thanks so much.

Tyrese: My pleasure. See you then.

Rene went downstairs and enjoyed the hotel's continental breakfast. She checked out, drove across the street to Starbucks, and purchased a grande vanilla chai latte with soy to help soothe her nerves. Rene then headed toward Lowe's. That was when she realized that she forgot to make a phone call before she left the hotel.

In order for the plan to work, Rene needed both Nina and Jalen at the house at the same time. She had not spoken to Nina since she left the house the day before, and she was not sure what Nina's work schedule was. She tried to track Nina's movements, but they were all over the place. Rene never knew when Nina was coming or going. Rene had to make sure that Nina would be home and she wouldn't get stuck entertaining Jalen all day. That would not be good for either of them.

Ring, ring.

Nina picked up. "Hey, what's up? You good? Did you come home last night? I was blowing you up. You didn't see my text messages?"

"Where are you?" asked Rene.

"I'm at the house. Wow. You just gon' blatantly ignore me? Damn, you can't answer my question?"

"OMG! Are you my probation officer now? No, I didn't come home last night. Are you leaving anytime soon?"

"Breathe easy and relax please. No need to be so snappy. Nah, I'm not going nowhere. I was supposed to pick Jacob up around seven, but Sheca ended up dropping him off. She had to take her mom to the hospital. Where was yo' ass at?"

"It's a long story that I can't get into right now. I'll tell you when I get home. I'm on my way now."

"Bet! Look at you out here livin' yo' best life! Yasss! It's about goddamn time. I'ma need all that tea, so hurry up and bring ya ass here!"

"I'll be there shortly. Bye."

Hearing Nina's voice lit a fuse in the pit of Rene's gut. She was getting so angry that she had started speeding without even realizing it. The nerve of Nina to act like everything was okay between them.

"This dumb bitch is thinking I was with a man," Rene said angrily. "I'm not her! Livin' my best life my ass! She's probably on the phone right now telling Jalen. 'About damn time' really meant, 'About damn time I'll be able to have Jalen to myself.' Stupid ho!" Rene pounded her fist into her armrest.

Knowing that she needed to calm down and regain her composure before she linked up with Tyrese, Rene let the window down and turned on some Earth, Wind & Fire. There was something about old-school R&B that mellowed Rene out almost instantly. She had been that way all her life. Her mom said that even when she was a toddler, if Rene was having a temper tantrum or fighting a nap, she could turn on some Isley Brothers or Anita Baker, and Rene would calm right down. That love for the music stuck with her and became a therapeutic method in her adult life.

As Rene turned into the Lowe's parking lot, she heard her phone ding. It was Tyrese letting her know where he was parked. Rene spotted his car and pulled into the parking space next to him.

"Thanks again for meeting me," Rene said as she greeted Tyrese with a hug.

"It's all good," Tyrese replied. "I'm a man of my word. You said you needed the photos, so here they are. These are copies of everything that the private investigator gave me." He handed Rene an envelope with her name on the front of it.

When the envelope hit Rene's hand, it was hard for her to hold it. It was almost as if she lost muscle control in that hand. She slowly opened the envelope and pulled one picture up halfway. Sure enough, there were Jalen and Nina walking in a parking lot sharing a laugh. Nina's hand was on Jalen's shoulder. Rene shook her head and shoved the picture back in the envelope.

"This is some major-league bullshit!" Rene mumbled through her teeth.

"Hey, hey, hey," Tyrese said, grabbing Rene's hand. "Look at me. Don't do that."

Rene was confused by that statement. "Do what?" she asked.

"Don't give them the power to change you. Whether it be something small like the course of your day or your mood at the moment, or something major like your integrity or character, don't allow them to control anything in your life. I know that is easier said than done, but trust me, keeping that mindset is going to keep you from going crazy and also from going to jail. Neither of them is worth those things happening. You're bigger than them and this situation. You just have to believe it. Mind over matter, my dear."

Rene knew Tyrese was right. However, being mentally tough in this type of situation was so ridiculously hard to do. Her emotions were at an all-time high, and it was getting harder and harder to control them.

"I get it and you're right. My dad has told me that my entire life. I'm so angry though! I can't help it. This is by far the most traumatic thing I have ever gone through in my life," Rene shared.

"Didn't your parents get a divorce when you were younger? I'm sure that was tough."

"That was different. I was sad at first, but when I saw how different and happy my mom and dad were once they were apart, that changed everything for me. I was just happy that they were happy. This drama with Jalen and Nina is completely different. This is directly affecting my life! Sometimes I wonder how in the world I am going to get through all of this and not need psychiatric help," Rene explained.

"Time will heal what your heart can't heal on its own," Tyrese encouraged her. "I have to get going. I have a few more stops I need to make and a little bit of money to make. You keep your head up, beautiful, and stay out of trouble. I don't want to see your picture on the eleven o'clock news or in my newsfeed on Facebook," he joked.

Rene managed to squeeze out a smile. "I'll be sure to do both. Thanks again." She held up the envelope. "You have no idea how much I appreciate this. You have been a huge help to me."

"It's nothing," replied Tyrese. He opened his car door and got in. "Don't be a stranger," he yelled before closing his door. Rene gave him a thumbs-up and waved goodbye.

She checked her phone to see what time it was. It said 10:52. *Damn! I need to hurry up!*

She quickly walked through Lowe's, grabbing three new door locks and a universal garage door opener. She paid for her items and practically ran to her car. On her way home, Rene remembered that there were a few grocery items they were out of that the kids would need. She texted Jalen and told him to come at eleven forty-five to give her a little more wiggle room. He texted back saying that was fine.

As Rene pulled into her driveway, she had to pause and say a little prayer, asking God to protect her from herself. "Lord, I have too much to lose. I have a successful career and two beautiful children who need me, and I am not about that jail life. I ask that you please be a fence around me so that I don't commit any acts that will cause me to lose everything I love. In your name I pray. Amen."

Her level of anger was boiling at 200 degrees, and it was almost like she was seeing red. Playing her music and saying her prayer was slowing bringing her back down. Then she saw in her rearview mirror Jalen pulling up behind her.

"It's show time!" she mumbled to herself. She popped her trunk and headed to the rear of her car.

"Wow. You look so beautiful," Jalen said with a huge smile on his face.

"Hello to you too," Rene responded.

"You need some help? I can grab those for you," Jalen offered, referring to the grocery bags in Rene's trunk.

"Sure," replied Rene in a dry tone. "I'll get everything in the back seat. You can get the bags in the trunk." Rene did not want Jalen to see what she had purchased from Lowe's or the Target bags that had the items she bought to stay at the hotel.

The two entered the house from the garage. Rene walked into the dining room and placed the bags that she'd carried in on the table.

"Where do you want these?" Jalen said as he held up the bags in his hands.

"Oh, you can just set those down on the kitchen counter," Rene instructed. "I'll put that stuff away in a minute. Thank you."

Jalen did as she asked. One of the bags broke, causing a carton of juice to hit the floor hard and make a loud noise.

"ReRe? Is that you down there?" Nina yelled down the stairs.

"Yep! It's me. Come down real quick," Rene yelled back.

"You scared the shit out of me. I didn't even hear the garage go up, so I had no clue you were here," Nina expressed. "Now bring ya ass on in the living room and have a seat. Let me here this long story you were talking about! Where have you been?" questioned Nina as she walked down the steps. Once she reached the bottom and saw Jalen standing there, she stopped dead in her tracks. She looked over at Rene with confusion clearly on her face.

"Why is he here?" Nina boldly asked.

"Where is Jacob?" Rene responded, ignoring Nina's inquiry.

"He's upstairs taking a nap. What's going on, Re—"

Wham! Rene ran over and punched Nina smack dead in the face. Nina quickly fell back onto the floor and grabbed her nose with her hands. Rene straddled Nina and let her fist go to work. It was almost like she transformed into another person. She kicked Nina in the stomach, grabbed her by the hair, and began to punch her over and over again in the face.

"You dirty, no-good bitch! I can't believe you would turn on me! You're nothing but a cheap, low-life gutter ho! I made you! I took care of you! Now I should kill you!" screamed Rene as she punched.

Jalen stood there stunned and in pure disbelief at what he was witnessing. Blood had started to flow from Nina's lip, mouth, nose, and forehead. Rene seemed to not care at all. She showed no mercy. The strangest thing about the fight was that Nina was not even trying to fight back. She managed to ball up and cover her head, but that was all.

Jalen ran over to attempt to break the two ladies up. After some serious tugging and pulling, he managed to drag Rene away. She swiftly turned around and smacked Jalen so hard his ears started ringing. She slapped him right across his face as hard as she could and then kneed him in the nuts.

"Ooohhhh shhhiiittt!" Jalen yelled out in pain as he fell to his knees. "What the hell is wrong with you?" he screamed at Rene as he buckled over in agony.

"What's wrong with *me?* What's wrong with *me?* You and your low-down, dirty-ass ways and this nasty hood-rat ho you've been messing around with! That's what's wrong with me! Oh yeah, I know everything, and I have photos to prove it!"

Jalen looked up at Rene, still in pain. His face clearly showed that he had no idea what Rene was talking about. "You are talking crazy!" Jalen responded. "You know that? And why in the fuck did you hit me?"

"Don't try that blank, dumbfounded shit with me! I had a little lunch meeting with Tyrese yesterday. He had a lot to say about Nina and a lot to say about you."

When Nina heard Rene say that she had met with Tyrese, she knew there was no turning back. She knew that what was to come could not be stopped.

"So what?" Jalen responded. "What does your meeting with Tyrese have to do with me? I don't know that dude, and he doesn't know me," Jalen yelled in an angry and disturbing voice. He was finally able to stand up straight.

"Really? You just gon' keep playing this role, huh?" asked Rene. "Before he put Nina's ass out on the street, he had her followed by a private investigator. He had pictures of you and her together! Leaving a hotel! Smiling and laughing and shit, sitting in a restaurant eating, going into clubs, all types of shit!"

Rene went into the dining room and grabbed the envelope off of the table. When she got back to Jalen and Nina, she pulled the pictures out of the envelope and threw the pictures at them. "Before you start lying, Tyrese provided proof!" Rene screamed.

"I almost forgot the icing on this fucked-up cake. Your little slut bucket over there," Rene said, pointing to Nina, who was still lying on the floor, "also confessed to Tyrese that you are Jacob's daddy!"

Jalen's face turned pale. His eyes were so big they looked like they might fall out of his head and onto the floor. His nostrils were flared, and he was staring at Rene, trying to speak but struggling to do so. His expression was one of a person who had witnessed a ghost walk through the door.

"I'm whose daddy? Jacob's?" Jalen asked. "Is that what the fuck you're saying this nigga told you?"

"You heard me!" Rene responded. "That's why Tyrese put her ass out. She's been telling this big-ass lie, pretending she didn't know why Tyrese did what he did. Truth is he found out all about your love fling and was not about to support another man's whore and baby. Between them pictures and her admitting it was all true, there is no way you are going to smooth-talk your way out of this one. How long had you planned on keeping up with this charade? Putting on this front? I can't believe you two are sitting around here, living your life with your secret family, enjoying each other but pretending to hate each other, all while I'm playing the role of your fool. All this time. All this time! Here I am, thinking I'm wifey, when in reality I'm the freaking mistress! My kids and I are the other family! Isn't that right, skank?" Rene said, looking toward Nina. She began to head back Nina's way.

Nina quickly jumped up with hopes of being able to defend herself if Rene was coming back for more. "Rene, please! Just wait a minute. You have to let me explain," begged Nina.

Rene looked at Nina with eyes that could kill. You would have thought that Nina had one horn coming out of her forehead and a tail out of her butt from the expression on Rene's face.

"Explain what, tramp? Explain how you've been sneaking around with my husband but claiming to be my friend? Explain how you moved into my house, knowing that your baby and my children have the same father? Oh no, wait, let me guess, you want to explain to me how you claim you love me and would kill anybody for bothering me, but you're the one with the knife in my back? Is that it, Nina? Is that what you want to explain? Did I get everything?"

Nina began to sob. "Please don't hate me. I didn't want you to find out this way. It wasn't something I planned. It just happened! I'm sorry!" she blurted out.

Jalen lifted his face and looked at Nina like he wanted to choke her with his bare hands. "Hold on, bitch! Nah, bae, she's lying! I haven't done anything with her! I never touched her! She and her ex are telling bald-faced lies. You are my wife, and there is no other woman! Jacob is not my baby!" Jalen said, defending himself. He walked over to Rene and stood in between her and Nina.

Jalen tried to reason with Rene. "Look, I don't know what the hell is going on here, but all this you're talking is crazy. I don't know what ol' dude told you, but I have never cheated on you. Not never. The only lie I have been keeping from you is . . . is . . ."

"Oh, for goodness' sake! Don't act all nervous and shook up now!" Rene interrupted.

"I had a gambling problem, okay?" Jalen quickly admitted.

Rene burst into laughter. "A gambling problem? Do I look like boo-boo the fool?" she asked.

"It's true, babe. I went to a few poker games with one of the guys who works for me, and I got hooked. One night, I saw Nina waitressing at one of the spots. We would always say hi or whatever, and over time we just got really cool. She said she knew a few other spots that were similar to the place she was working at. She thought I might like to go, and I agreed. She would take me to all the hot poker halls and underground poker games. That's probably how he got those pictures. I was in a really bad place during that time. That's why my business wasn't doing well for so long. I was gambling all the money away. I had a problem, but I got help. That's the entire story! Nina told me that she said something to Tyrese about me gambling, and that's why I was a little nervous when you said you talked to him. That's why I didn't want Nina living here. Between the incidents at the club that night, and her knowing about the gambling problem, I knew her being around would be trouble. She is so damn ghetto and evil. I just didn't want her around. Shut your mouth, bitch! You're a coldhearted liar," Jalen yelled at Nina. "You're lying and you know it. I have never touched you. And that baby is not mine!"

"I cannot believe you are standing there saying this! We never hooked up, Jalen? Not ever? Jacob is not yours?" asked Nina angrily. "If that's the case, then why is his name Jacob? I named him after you at your request! You wanted all of your kids to have names that start with J, like you. After all I have done for you, keeping everything a secret, having your back when she didn't . . . Now that the cat is out of the bag, you wanna deny me? You promised we would be together!" Nina became enraged. She tried to lunge toward Jalen, but Rene knocked her back down.

"Oh, you can forget about that! The only one swinging on anybody up in here is me!" Rene said to Nina as she attempted to get off the floor for a second time.

Rene turned to address Jalen. "Just admit it. Be a man and tell me you did it. Why are you going through all of this, playing all of these games? You've been caught! The jig is up, game over, clock expired, wave the white flag already. For once in your life, man up! You got busted!"

"It's not true, Rene! Do you hear me? It's not true!" Jalen yelled back at her.

"Yes, it is!" Nina screamed back at Jalen. "I can't believe you are doing this to us. What about all those times you said you loved me? What about the promise you made that we were goin' to be a family? What about our son? Jalen, please stop all of this!"

Jalen looked at Nina with disbelief. "Oh, my goodness! You are straight-up crazy! You need professional help and some medication. Rene, baby, please! You have to believe me."

Rene stood there frozen. With all the evidence she'd presented and Nina pleading with him not to leave her, how could he still be denying the whole thing?

"Do I look like an idiot?" Rene said to Jalen with a puzzled look on her face. "Have I been that big of a dummy during our marriage that you think you can tell me any old thing and I'll believe you?"

"No. It's because you're my wife and I'm your husband that I think you should believe me," clarified Jalen. "Things look bad, but look at where it's coming from. Are you ready to throw our lives and marriage in the trash based on some punk-ass clown and a lying hood-rat whore?"

"A what?" Nina cried. "I'm a lying hood rat? You shouldn't treat the mother of your child that way. You're happy Rene is your wife now? You said you had fallen out of love with her. That you only loved me! That you and I and what we have is what was important to you. Jalen, you told me that Rene was just a gravy train you were using to get your business where you wanted it to be. I don't understand! Please, Jalen!" Nina pleaded again.

Jalen's words were starting to penetrate Rene. Rene had watched Nina tell lies in the past, tears and all, and then laugh about the situation later. When it came to something that she wanted, she would go to any extreme to make it happen. The overflow of different stories was so overwhelming.

What Jalen was saying didn't make any sense. What Nina was saying was making a whole lot of sense. Now she was pleading with him not to leave her and their son? That wasn't how Nina did things, which further had Rene convinced that Jalen was lying.

"You know what, Jalen?" began Rene. "I am pretty sure that the truth is somewhere in between both of your cluttered messes. Bottom line, you lied to me, and you're probably still lying to me right now. I don't want anything else to do with you. I don't even know who you are anymore. Either you have been having an affair with my best friend, or you were sneaking around with her, gambling our money away. Whichever it is, you're not the man I married. Nina seems to know more about the real Jalen than I do. An outside person! You made a vow to me. For better or for worse, sickness and health, thick or thin! You violated those vows! I'm not doing this dance with you anymore. You don't have to continue to live a double life because I'm setting you free. What you do need to do is get the rest of your crap and get out of my house today!"

"Your house?" Jalen asked.

"That's right, Negro, my house!" Rene repeated. "Oh, and you will be hearing from my lawyer. I want a divorce!"

To hear Rene say those words made Jalen's soul shrink down to nothing. What just happened? He could not lose Rene, and he refused to bow out so easily.

"I'll get my things if that's what you really want, but don't think for one second that this is it," replied Jalen. "I'm not losing my kids, and I'm not losing you. Before it's all said and done, you will know the truth. If after you know and understand the truth, you still want a divorce, I'll give it to you. But as long as you are believing a lie, I will continue to fight."

Rene gave Jalen a cold look and rolled her eyes. "Sound good, but while you're doing all this fighting and talking, please start walking up the stairs to get your stuff. 'Cause quite frankly, I'm tired of looking at you," Rene boldly stated to Jalen.

Jalen stared at Rene while she stared back. He decided not to say anything else and just get upstairs to start packing his things.

As Jalen began to walk up the steps, Nina leaned to the side to let him by and mumbled, "Oh, so you can fight to keep her but not me. You can sit me out on the curb like I'm garbage or something like it's nothing? You're going to wish you were dead by the time I'm done with you."

Jalen was furious. He couldn't believe that Nina had the balls to even say two words to him, let alone spew off threats. Before he knew it, he'd rushed back down the stairs and backhanded Nina across her cheek.

"Shut up! Just shut the fuck up! You are a psycho! I hate you! If you come anywhere near me or my family again, you won't have to wish you were dead because you will be, bitch!"

Jalen's behavior startled Rene. She had never seen him so angry and definitely had never seen him put his hands on a woman. It was like watching the Hulk transform.

"Jalen!" shouted Rene. "That is enough. Get away from her. Go upstairs and get your things so you can go!"

Jalen cut his eyes at Rene but didn't say a word. He turned around and did what he was told. He headed up the stairs.

"I thought he was going to kill me," Nina said, holding the left side of her face. "Rene, I promise I never meant to hurt you. I do love you. You are all Jacob and I have."

"Correction, bitch," Rene quickly interrupted. "I'm all Jacob has. You have nothing and no one. You need to get your coat and shoes and get the hell out of this house immediately!"

Nina was stunned. "Wait, what about my stuff? And look at my face. You just gon' put me out all bloody and bruised like this?"

"Girl! I guess you really are crazy." Rene chuckled. "Do you really think I give a rat's ass about your bruised and bloodied face? No! I don't. I don't care about you or anything that has to do with you except for that baby boy."

"Well, where am I supposed to go, Rene? I can't just be wandering the streets with a baby and a bunch of bags."

"You can't and you won't. You see, you are the only one leaving. Jacob is staying here. That means you will be wandering the streets with just you and a bunch of bags. Come back tomorrow around noon. All of your stuff will be sitting outside in garbage bags for you to load up in that piece of junk you call a car. Make sure your dumb ass is on time. I would hate for the community maintenance men to think all of your crap is trash and take it to the dumpster," Rene said sarcastically.

"What do you mean, Jacob is staying here? You can't take my baby from me!" said Nina boldly to Rene. "Are you crazy?"

"No, I'm quite sane. Are you really that selfish and stupid? You are going to drag him around from couch to couch to prove a point? I don't think so. He is staying right here with me. Again, get your coat, get your shoes, and get out!" said Rene as she pointed to the door.

Nina could hear the anger in Rene's voice and knew that it wasn't wise to keep debating with her. Although she really didn't want to, she grabbed her purse, jacket, and running shoes, and left the house.

Right before she walked out the door, she turned to Rene and said, "No matter what happens, know that my love for you has been and always will be real. I'm sorry. I hope one day you can forgive me." She lowered her head, walked out the door, and closed it behind her.

When Nina finally closed the door, Rene almost instantly got weak, like someone knocked the wind out of her. She slid down the wall onto the floor. Her life was crumbling before her eyes, and there was nothing she could do to stop it. Rene had never felt more helpless in her life. She pulled her knees to her chest, laid her head on top of them, and began crying her heart out.

Rene quickly had gone from wife to mistress and from friend to fool. The thought of it all made her heart ache. No matter how she tried to word it, things would never be the same.

After a few minutes had passed, she heard Jacob crying. She wiped her face with her shirt, hopped up, and went upstairs. By the time she got to Nina's room, she could smell why Jacob was crying.

"Ooh-wee, li'l guy! You are too small to smell this bad," she lovingly joked with the baby.

When Rene reached inside Jacob's crib to pick him up, he saw her face and began to laugh. He reached his arms out to her. She couldn't help but smile. He was just the cutest baby you ever wanted to see and so precious.

Rene changed his diaper, washed him up, and got him dressed. Although she hated to admit that she was doing it, she started to examine his facial features to see if he resembled Jalen or her kids at all. He did have Jalen's nose, but many babies had pudgy noses. And he had light eyes like Jalen and Jalen Jr., but Nina's grandmother had those eyes too.

"I don't know," Rene whispered to herself. "Who's your daddy, little man?"

"It's not me," Jalen responded, startling Rene.

"Ugh, get out already!" she yelled at him.

"Rene, I know you are mad, but I promise you, when this is all over, you will see that I'm not lying to you. I have done some wrong things, and I can own up to them. Having that baby with your best friend is not one of them."

"Okay. Got it. Now you have said what you need to say, so get steppin'!" Rene snapped at him.

Jalen just sighed and turned toward the steps. "Just do me this one favor. Never forget that I love you, and I'll never stop loving you. You are the love of my life."

Rene shook her head and threw her hands in the air. "What? Are you and that trick reading from the same 'Apologies for Suckers' handbook?" she asked Jalen. "I don't want to hear that shit! If you loved me so much, then we wouldn't be going through any of this, now would we? Get your ass down the steps and out of my house!"

Jalen's eyes began to get low and fill with water. He turned and walked slowly down the steps. Once Rene heard the door close, she looked out of the bedroom window and watched Jalen pull off. She looked at the chubby baby boy who was smiling and drooling in her arms.

"Well, little fella, looks like it's just you and me."

Rene was pretty sure that Nina thought she had one up on her, being that she didn't ask for the house key back. "Hmm, joke's on her stupid ass." Rene laughed to herself.

She put Jacob in his walker, grabbed the Lowe's bag, and began to change the locks on her front, back, and garage doors. Once she finished with that, she fixed something to eat and fed Jacob. Soon after, Jacob fell asleep in his highchair. Rene laid him down in his crib.

Rene had really put some thought into keeping Jacob. Even though he may be the love child who was the product of her husband's affair, she still loved him dearly and did not want anything to ever happen to him. He was just an innocent child who'd never asked for Nina to be his mom or to be born in such a messed-up situation. If Nina was bouncing around from place to place, Jacob would surely get the short end of the stick. She couldn't live with herself if he suffered even one day because she put him out with his no-good mama.

She also realized that by taking him in, she was taking on the responsibility of being his sole provider.

She couldn't force Jalen to take a DNA test because she wasn't Jacob's mother. Since he was denying that he was the father, she was pretty sure he wouldn't volunteer any support. Nina's working situation was good for the moment, but who knew how long that would last? Not to mention it seemed like every little dime she made from working went to shoes, clothes, and nights out in the bars. She had three cars get repossessed in a three-year period. That was how irresponsible Nina was. Chances were slim she would even try to fight to get Jacob back, but all of that was okay with Rene.

The night before, while she was in the hotel, she was able to really put things in perspective and make some crucial decisions. She enrolled Jacob in a different day-care and took Nina's name off of the kids' emergency cards at school. These moves meant Nina had no way of getting to any of the kids without raising some eyebrows.

While Jacob was asleep, Rene changed the code on her garage and garage door opener. This was necessary because Jalen had the old opener, but Rene did not want him to be able to come in and out of the house whenever he wanted to.

Now only she had access to the house. Hopefully this meant she would not have any surprise pop-ups or visitors waiting for her when she got home. Now how was she going to explain all of this to her kids?

Chapter 9

Unbelievable

A couple of months had passed, and Rene was doing the best she could to keep her and the kids' lives as normal as possible. She sat down with her boss and explained that her living situation had changed, and she didn't have the same amount of support that she had previously. He was more than understanding and agreed to let her work three days in the office and two days at home. Rene was very grateful to him and agreed to work one Saturday every month and two late nights a month, meaning she'd get off work at seven. Her mom agreed to take care of the kids on those days.

Rene took Nina's bed down, moved Jacob's crib and dresser into her room, set up a desk and her computer in Nina's old room, and turned it into her office. It all worked out great. On the days she worked from home, she had everything she needed there.

Jalen kept his word. Every chance he got, he tried to butter Rene up. He sent her flowers, had lunch delivered to her job, and he even left notes in the mailbox or in the kids' suitcases when they would come to visit, knowing Rene would be the one to unpack their luggage.

There were times she would get to work and there would be a voicemail from him, telling her to have a good day and that he missed her. To Rene's dismay, Jalen was still denying everything about the affair. He continued to say he had a gambling addiction and Nina was pretty much his dealer. She was the one feeding him information about the different poker spots. Jalen even offered to take Rene to some of the places that he and Nina went to together. She politely declined. She was trying to move on and encouraged him to do the same. He also politely declined.

In spite of Rene's constant rejections, Jalen kept fighting for his wife. Nina was doing a little fighting of her own, but definitely not in the same manner.

Rene was getting phone calls—tons of phone calls. Most of the time, the person just held the phone, not saying a word. Other times, the caller would blurt out random and stupid threats or phrases: "It ain't over 'til it's over," "Don't be a fool," "Only a stupid bitch would take care of a baby who belongs to her husband's side chick," and so on and so on.

At first Rene laughed at the anonymous callers. One time she had to giggle, and she asked the caller, "What is this, high school? Grow up and get a life." But that did no good, and the calls kept coming. Then she started getting text messages, sometimes ten or fifteen a day, from random and, Rene found out later, fake numbers.

Please don't give up on me.

I need you.

Just say you still love me.

You will regret this.

Jalen doesn't love you.

You are as dumb as they come.

Rene's first thought was that the calls were coming from Jalen. When she called to question him about it, he played dumb, like he didn't have a clue about what she was saying. Rene cussed him out anyway just in case he was lying. It didn't change anything. Jalen still didn't have a clue what she was talking about.

"Stop playing with me, Jalen. This stupidity is getting on my nerves! What? You still mad because I won't fall for your fairy tales?"

"Rene, think about it. Like really think about it," Jalen responded.

"I have thought about it!" Rene confirmed. "The messages that are coming to my phone and the time of day all point back to you."

"To be so smart, you're not that smart," Jalen joked.

"What did you say to me?" Rene asked, not seeing any humor in the situation at all.

"Okay. Stop. Like seriously," Jalen said. "Didn't you say that the texts and phone calls have been coming from several different fake numbers?"

"Yes. What's your point?" Rene answered.

"How in the hell would I know how to do that? I still haven't figured out how to use all the features on my phone or properly respond to a comment on Instagram. But I'm the guy creating fake phone numbers? Come on, Rene."

Rene couldn't help but laugh. "Damn," she said. "You're right. You are definitely by far the most technically challenged person I know. It took you over a week to figure out how to use the camera on your phone and another week to figure out how to send a picture in a text message."

Jalen joined Rene in laughing at his poor technical skills. "Oh, you got jokes I see. So what? I figured it out. That's all that matters," Jalen said proudly. "It's good to hear that laugh of yours. I haven't heard it in a long time."

"Oh, goodness! Yeah, yeah. Goodbye, ugly," Rene said, still laughing.

"You have a good night, ma'am," Jalen wished Rene.

When she got off the phone, Rene sat back on her couch and took a nice big gulp of wine. It felt so good to share that laugh with Jalen. She missed those moments. He always knew how to put a smile on her face even during a bad situation. She was starting to miss Jalen's presence. Her bed was getting extremely cold and lonely. When he came to get the kids, she would find herself daydreaming about better days, when her family was one and she had her husband at home with her every night. She missed laying her head on his chest at night. It seemed as though their heartbeats followed each other, creating a perfect melody. His kisses would send a shiver down her back and sometimes even make her get a little moist in her tender spot. Even after all the years they had been together, Jalen still made her feel what she felt the first time they made love. Now those days were gone.

Rene knew that she would have times when she missed Jalen. She was prepared for them and ready to face them head-on. She continued to drink her wine and relax on the couch. Rene took out her journal and began to write. Writing was therapeutic for her, especially during times like these.

> *Finding out your husband has another family and has them living with you and your children has the potential to drive any woman crazy. Missing that man can create a feeling of worthlessness. How is it possible to miss such an awful person? It's normal. Bad acts do not instantly remove love, history, or memories. One day at a time. That's all people can do: allow their hearts and minds to heal one day at a time.*

She often wondered what the future would be like and if she could continue to make it alone. She was always able to say a prayer and keep the wheels turning. The kids sometimes would ask if Daddy could come spend the night or if Jacob could go with them on their visits. Rene was able to keep her answers creative without totally telling a lie.

One day when Jalen was dropping the kids off, Rene noticed he wasn't driving his truck. "What's up with the Malibu? Definitely not how you roll. Where's your truck?" asked Rene.

"Seems someone decided it would look better with a brick through two of the windows and all four tires flat. This is a rental. I'm keeping it until my truck is ready," answered Jalen.

"Oh, my! Clutch my pearls!" Rene said as she grabbed her neck, pretending to clutch an invisible pearl necklace. "Are you serious? Do you think it was your baby mama?" she asked in a sarcastic voice and with a smirk on her face.

"I'm really not in the mood for your sarcasm," Jalen warned her. "I just had to come out of two thousand dollars plus a towing fee. And for your information, my baby mama is standing in front of me. So, does that mean you did it? If you did, I'll call the detective and have him come arrest you right now."

"Yeah, whatever," Rene replied in a sassy voice. "I have better things to do with my time than go back and forth with you. Being that I have to take care of my kids plus someone else's."

Jalen shook his head. "That someone else is Nina. Not me. With ya smart-ass mouth."

"I need to know something. If you get a DNA test and the results say that he is your baby, can I get some child support?" asked Rene.

"Hell no! There is not a test on earth that will ever say I'm the father," Jalen quickly stated.

"You still getting prank calls?" asked Rene.

"Yep, you?" responded Jalen.

"Unfortunately. I'm about ninety percent sure it's your baby mama and some of her ghetto friends doing it though. They even have started sending me emails and Facebook messages from fake pages. These hoes have way too much time on their hands."

Jalen was in disbelief. "That's messed up. And would you please stop calling that psycho my baby mama? She is not my baby anything. Since we're asking questions, I have one for you."

Rene was intrigued. "I'm listening. What is it?"

"When the truth is finally unveiled and you see that I wasn't lying, am I going to be able to get my side of the bed back?" Jalen asked as he tugged on the bottom of Rene's shirt.

Rene began to blush. "Ha. Now you're the one with jokes. I'm really not trying to go there with you right now. I'll believe it when and if it should come to pass. Not a second sooner. Fool me once, shame on you. Fool me twice, shame on me. Fool me three times, yeah, now I got to cut you!"

Jalen laughed at Rene's wannabe tough attitude. Through all the madness that had taken place, she still was the most beautiful woman in the world to him. Her smile and stunning presence made him want to fight harder and harder to get back in her good graces.

"Okay, beautiful. I hear you," Jalen affectionately replied.

As the two were finishing their conversation, Rene's cell phone rang. Her caller ID read Restricted. It was another unidentified caller, her twelfth call of the day. Rene flashed the phone to Jalen. He motioned for her to go ahead and answer it.

"This is Rene."

"Tell that no-good son of a bitch that there is more where that came from."

"Tell him yourself, skank! I know this is you, Nina. Why don't you grow up and get a freaking life?"

"I'm coming to get what's mine. Everything that's mine!"

Rene quickly changed her tone from angry to furious. "Who are you yelling at, bitch? The only thing that was yours was them raggedy, cheap-ass Simply Fashion clothes that I put on the street when you left. Other than that, there's nothing here for ya!"

"Fuck that shit. I'm talking about my son and my heart."

"Your son is now my son! What the hell do you mean, your heart? What does that mean?"

Before Rene got a response, the phone hung up and Nina was no longer on the other end. Rene was visibly annoyed and pissed off. She was sick of Nina and her antics. Rene didn't understand how this chick could cause so much commotion in someone else's world and then make them feel like they were the victim.

Soon after the phone call ended, Jalen got a text saying, You don't deserve her. You will never get her back. I'm going to do everything I can to make sure of it. She's too good for you.

"You just had to screw around with a psycho chick, huh?" asked Rene.

"Chill out, Rene! I'm not going to keep asking you to watch your mouth! I have never screwed around with her or anybody else. You act like you want it all to be true. Honestly, I'm not in the mood for your pity party right now, so shut up!" As soon as the words left Jalen's lips, he regretted saying them.

"Pity party? Negro, you have got to be all outside of your mind talking to me like that. Are you serious right now? You know what? Never mind. It's time for you to get gone," Rene insisted.

"I'm sorry, Rene," Jalen quickly said.

"You got that right. You are one sorry muthafucka. Leave!" said Rene as she walked away. She walked into the garage, and when she got to the house door, she closed the garage.

Jalen stood in the driveway trying to think of something to say, but nothing was coming to him quickly enough. When he got in his car, a text message came through his phone. Hoping it was Rene, he quickly grabbed it out of his pocket and read it. The message said, I told you. You'll never get her back.

Rene was finishing up her work and getting ready to head home for the evening when her cell phone started buzzing. "Damn. Not this crap again," she said to herself when she didn't recognize the number. "Hello!" she answered, not hiding her major attitude.

"Oh, okay. Hello to you too, gorgeous. Did I catch you at a bad time?" said the deep voice on the other end.

"Ty . . . Tyrese?" Rene hesitated.

"Yes, ma'am. It is I and I am he," Tyrese replied jokingly. "What's going on with you? I haven't heard from you since I saw you at Lowe's that day. I wanted to make sure you were doing okay. How's everything going?"

Rene was at a loss for words. The sound of Tyrese's sexy voice had her in a daze. Imagining his perfect face left her speechless. She almost didn't hear his question.

"Oh, uh, yeah. You know, I'm hanging in there. Everything just has been so different since I put Jalen and Nina out. Having three kids and trying to keep things in order is a challenge. What number is this you're calling me from? I almost didn't answer."

"It's my second cell. I use it mainly for work. My other phone died. Wait, three kids?" Tyrese asked, somewhat confused. "I thought you only had two."

"I do. Two biological children. I decided to keep Jacob, Nina's little boy, too. I think it was for the best," Rene explained.

"Really? I mean, with Nina's history and jacked-up ways, you're probably right," Tyrese agreed. "That was very honorable of you. I don't know if many people could have done that."

"Yeah, I know. My mom thinks I'm crazy, but she is still supportive. She always says to me, 'Girl, if God don't bless you for this one, He must be on vacation!' He's a really sweet baby though. If it weren't for him and my kids, this whole ordeal would be a lot harder to handle than what it is. They keep me going," said Rene.

"Wow. I always knew you were a remarkable woman, but never like this. You have to let me take you out to dinner and maybe a movie. You deserve a little break," offered Tyrese.

"Dinner and a movie?" Rene asked in a doubtful tone. "I think that's pushing it a bit. I'm not trying to go out on a date with you, or anyone for that matter."

"Okay, I get it. How about just dinner? We can drive separate cars, restaurant of your choice. How does that sound? Is that cool?"

Rene started thinking. She would love to get some free time. She had been so wrapped up in making sure that the kids adjusted well, ensuring that her crazy personal life did not interfere with work, and dealing with all of the drama from Nina and her friends, her tension and stress levels were sky high.

"Okay. I'll go. Only if my mom will watch the kids for me though. If she says yes, you got a deal," Rene replied.

"That's what's up! Let her know I'll pay her if she wants me to!"

Rene laughed. "You are so crazy! It's my mother! Not the neighbor's teenage daughter."

"I'm serious," Tyrese assured her.

"Okay, I'll let her know, and I'll get back to you," promised Rene.

"I look forward to it. You have a wonderful night, Mrs. Martin."

"Thanks. You do the same, Mr. Smalls."

When Rene ended the call, she had the biggest smile on her face. The thought of seeing Tyrese and his fine, edible self would make any woman's cheeks turn red. She was really hoping her mom was free to watch the kids.

Once she was home, Rene got the kids fed, bathed, and into bed. She then called her mom. After sharing a few laughs, she asked her if she could watch the kids Friday night.

"Oh, are you and Jalen going on a date? You finally believe him. Amen! I knew that old raggedy, no-good Nina was lying. I told you I never liked the cut of her skirt. She has demon eyes, and she reeked of the streets! That is so wonderful, baby! I'm glad you finally came to your senses," Ms. Martha praised.

"Mom!" Rene interrupted. "Calm down. I'm not going anywhere with Jalen. I still don't believe him. Nothing has changed."

"What? Aw, shoot! Well, where are you going then? More importantly, with whom are you going?" Ms. Martha asked in a stern voice.

"Just to dinner with an old friend, Mama. I won't be out late or anything. I called because I was wondering if you could watch all the kids . . . including Jacob," Rene hesitantly asked.

Rene wasn't too sure how her mom would respond to that. She had a very strict "your mess is your mess" policy that she was quick to enforce when she thought any of her children were looking for her to get involved in difficult situations or bail them out of something that they created being dumb.

"Of course I will, baby girl. You know I don't believe in treating children differently. When your kids are here, all they talk about is their little cousin Jacob and what new thing he is learning to do. If you love him as your own, Rene, then he is a part of this family. So yes, they can all come. Bring them around six thirty. I should be done cooking dinner about that time, so I can feed them their supper. Oh, and be sure to bring that baby's walker. You know I don't do a whole bunch of carrying. My arms aren't as strong as they used to be."

"Yes, ma'am," answered Rene. "I will make sure I do that. Thank you so much, Mama. Your words mean the world to me. I'll see you on Friday. I love you."

"I love you too, baby."

When Friday came around, Rene was excited and nervous all at the same time. She could barely sleep the night before. Going out to a nice dinner and holding a conversation with an adult was something she had not experienced in a while.

Although she was looking forward to seeing Tyrese, she couldn't help but think about Jalen and how he might feel. She didn't want him to know. Not because she was worried about saving her marriage, but because she knew if he found out, he would automatically think she was trying to seek revenge or have a fling of her own, and that just was not the case. If she did something like that, she would be no better than Nina. Rene was standing firm on that.

Rene's day got off to a great start. The kids woke up and got dressed with no problems. Her daughter helped her get the baby dressed, which gave her a little more time to fix her hair and pack the kids' lunches. She left the house ten minutes early, and there was no traffic on her route to work. To top it all off, when she opened her office door, there sat a vase of roses being hugged by a teddy bear, and a bag with EDIBLE ARRANGEMENTS on the front of it.

"What is all of this?" Rene asked her assistant.

"They were delivered bright and early. I had just taken my coat off when the delivery guy came in," Rene's assistant shared.

Rene went to her desk and read the card aloud. "'Lovely flowers for a lovely lady. I can't wait to lay my eyes on you this evening. I hope you have an incredible day. Yours truly, Tyrese.'"

Rene could have hit the floor. What a wonderful, sweet, and thoughtful gesture. Tyrese was really turning up the heat. When she took the Edible Arrangements box out of the bag and saw the chocolate-dipped apples and strawberries, the biggest smile ever stretched across her face. These were her absolute favorites.

Rene managed to make it through her day without doing a cartwheel or jumping in the air and clicking her heels together out of excitement. She finished her last report, logged out of her computer, and jumped into her car. The kids' bags were already packed, so when she went home, all she had to do was get ready for the evening.

She found a sexy purple maxi dress that fell off the shoulders, and she chose purple and black heels to match. She curled her hair in big curls, and then swooped it up, leaving pieces hanging in the front and back. After she added the finishing touches to her makeup, she was ready to roll.

She packed the kids up and took them to her mom's. She was standing in her mother's kitchen setting up Jacob's walker when her mom got a chance to look her up and down.

"You sure are pretty jazzed up to be going to dinner with an old friend, don't you think? Sexy dress, seductive hair, a little extra makeup. Look at you," Ms. Martha commented.

Rene sighed. "It's not like that, Mama. We are having dinner at a pretty upscale restaurant, so I had to dress accordingly. That's all. I promise."

"Mm-hmm," grunted Ms. Martha. "If you say so. You just remember this right here: your mess—"

"Is my mess. I know, Ma, I know. Thanks again for keeping the kids." Rene kissed Ms. Martha on the cheek, kissed all of the kids good-bye, and headed on her way.

When she reached the parking lot, her phone rang. Assuming it was Tyrese, she quickly answered it without looking at the caller ID. "Hello."

"Rene, it's me. Please don't hang up. I really need to talk to you. I miss—"

Click! Rene hung up the phone as soon as she recognized Nina's voice. "She is not about to ruin my night," Rene confirmed to herself. Rene got out of her car and began to walk toward the restaurant.

Tyrese was standing at the door waiting for her. "Oh, my! Wow! You are absolutely breathtaking!" he complimented her.

Once again, Tyrese was making Rene blush like a high school freshman talking to the captain of the football team. "Well, thank you. You don't look so bad yourself," Rene returned.

That was the PG-13 version of what she was thinking. She really wanted to say, "If we weren't in public, I would snatch your clothes off and jump your bones right now! Or at least take you in the bathroom and do a few things to you." She was pretty sure what actually did come out of her mouth was a little more appropriate.

They embraced, and Tyrese extended his arm to her. "Shall we?" he asked.

Rene smiled and put her arm around his. "Yes, we shall."

Tyrese opened the door, and the two entered the restaurant. Tyrese had made a reservation, so they were seated rather quickly. A waiter wearing a white collared dress shirt and black tie came to their table. He placed two glasses of Rene's favorite wine and menus on their table.

"Wait. This is one of my favorites. How did you know?" Rene asked, totally surprised.

"I am a very observant man. That's all. When I called and made the reservation, I asked them to make a note that we would like two glasses of pinot noir when we were seated," Tyrese shared.

"Impressive," Rene replied. "I will admit, that was pretty dope. So was the gift that you had delivered to my office. Thank you! I enjoyed every bit."

Tyrese let out a light laugh. "I'm glad."

The waiter returned with bread and butter and took their orders. He soon returned with a Caesar salad for Rene and a cup of seafood bisque for Tyrese.

Rene began to explain the whole saga of drama that had come into her life: the fight she had with Nina, Jalen's version of events, Nina pretty much stalking them both, and everything in between.

"You know, Rene, I'm going to kick myself later for saying this, but there may be some truth to Jalen's story," said Tyrese.

Rene looked surprised. "Say what? Come again? Not you too! You sound like my mother."

Tyrese laughed. "I'm sorry, I really am, but . . . now that I think about it, one of the clubs they were at is also a small pool hall. They have a mini casino in the basement. There are a lot of dice and poker games that go on there."

"Really? Are you sure? How do you know this?" questioned Rene.

"My dad's youngest brother has a little gambling problem himself. My cousins and I have had to pull him out of there on numerous occasions. Don't get me wrong, I'm not saying that Jalen and Nina weren't knocking boots, or that Jalen is totally innocent, but there is a legit possibility that the whole gambling story may not be a lie. It's just something to consider," Tyrese clarified.

"As if I didn't have enough stuff going on in my head—" Before Rene could finish her sentence, she heard the hostess yelling across the room.

"Excuse me, ma'am! Excuse me! You can't walk back there! Ma'am, please, you must have a reservation or leave your name with me!"

All of a sudden, Tyrese blurted out, "Ah, hell no! What is she doing here?"

When Rene turned around in her chair, she saw Nina stomping through the restaurant with the hostess and two waiters hot on her trail.

"Rene! Rene!" Nina began to scream. "I just need to talk with you please! Please! Rene!"

Rene was so stunned. Even though her brain was telling her to talk, she couldn't get anything to come out.

"Get away from here! Call security or the police right now!" Tyrese ordered the restaurant staff.

"You shut up! What are you doing here with her? Are you trying to take her from me too?" Nina shouted at Tyrese.

That statement threw Rene far off into left field. "What do you mean, take me from you? You don't own me, Nina! I'm not your puppet. You don't pull the strings and I do and say what you want me to. Nobody is taking me from anything or anyone. When you decided to sleep around with my husband, you pushed me away. And for the last time, leave me alone! Forget you even know me! Kick rocks and figure it out! Stop with all the phone calls!

Stop with all the text messages! Stop getting your stupid-ass friends to do shit! Just stop! I'm done with you. You're invisible to me," Rene yelled at Nina.

Nina fell to her knees. She was crying so hard she could barely catch her breath. "But what about our friendship? Our sisterhood? I love you! You are my world! Can't you see that I'm sorry? Can't you see that? Please, can you forgive me? I did it all for you. Jalen doesn't deserve you. Nobody does!"

While Nina was on the floor, the two waiters managed to grab her by her arms and drag her out of the restaurant.

"This is so embarrassing," Rene said as she finished off her glass of wine in one big gulp.

"It's all right. It's not your fault. You okay?" Tyrese asked as he rubbed Rene's hand.

Rene nodded. "I will be. I just need to calm down. Can I have another glass of wine please? Then let's just eat and get out of here."

"Absolutely!" said Tyrese as he motioned for their waiter to come to the table.

They quickly finished their meal, and Tyrese paid the check. As they walked outside, Tyrese put his arm around Rene and pulled her to him. "Don't lose your cool over this. Keep your head up. Things will get better," he encouraged Rene. He then kissed her on the forehead.

Rene smiled. "Thanks. That is the plan. Hopefully I can find the strength to stick to it."

Once they reached the parking lot, Tyrese and Rene hugged and said goodbye. Both turned to go to their cars. All of a sudden, Rene heard Tyrese yell out, "No, no, no! Not my baby! Man, what the fuck! No, this crazy bitch didn't!"

Rene's heart almost jumped out of her chest. She ran to see what was wrong. The closer she got, she could see why Tyrese was yelling and cursing. Tyrese's car had white spray paint all over it, the front windows were busted out, and the two back tires were flat.

"Oh, my God!" Rene ran to Tyrese. "I'm so sorry! I'm calling the police right now!"

Rene stayed with Tyrese until the police got there. It was getting late, and she had to get to her mom's to get the kids. Tyrese said he was okay and for her to go ahead and leave.

Rene could not believe all the drama taking place in her life. She never asked for any of this. It was starting to feel like she was being punished for Nina and Jalen's wrongdoing. She could honestly and wholeheartedly say that she had done nothing to deserve any of the crap that was happening to her.

On the way home from her mom's, Tyrese called. "Hey, lady? Are you okay?"

"I'm fine. The real question is, are you okay? What happened with your car?"

"To be totally transparent, no, I'm not okay. I have never been so pissed off in my life! I can't believe this psycho bitch messed up my baby."

"Are you sure it was Nina?"

"When the police got there, they were able to pull the surveillance video from the restaurant's cameras. The video tape showed Nina doing the entire thing. Right before she came inside the restaurant."

Rene let out a huge sigh. "Are you freaking kidding me? Wow! I am so sorry she did that to your car. What is this broad's malfunction?"

"I don't know. But what I have realized is everything she does seems to revolve around you. You are her motivation for the madness she creates. I'm getting a personal protection order on her, and I suggest you do the same. Watch your back, and don't take her behavior lightly."

"A PPO? On Nina? I don't think it's that serious. She will calm down eventually. I've seen her go through phases like this before."

"If you say so."

Chapter 10

The Letter with the Bloodstained Tears

Rene tossed and turned all night long. She could not believe that Nina was behaving the way she was. Rene had never seen her this emotional and out of control. The look in Nina's eyes at the restaurant haunted Rene in her dreams. Nina looked like a deranged psychopath who was off her meds and out of her mind.

If what Nina said was true, why was she so obsessed with Rene? Shouldn't she be taking her frustrations and anger out on Jalen? He was the one who used her, got her pregnant, and was now treating her like crap. Rene wasn't doing anything that any woman in her situation would do. Nina was lucky that Rene wasn't the one going ballistic, having temper tantrums, and destroying property. She should have been the one tearing stuff up, not Nina.

Thinking about all of the madness that Nina was putting Rene through started to make her blood pressure boil over. If Nina loved Rene the way she claimed she did, then why continue to harass her and make her life miserable? Why keep making things more and more difficult? On top of that, why was she so concerned with what Rene was doing and who she was doing it with, instead of being concerned about getting her son and taking care of him?

"That's it," Rene said as she jumped out of bed. "If drama is what she wants, then drama is what she is going to get."

In order for Rene to get all her ducks in a row, she was going to have to get Jalen on her team, which meant she was going to have to tell him about her dinner date with Tyrese and listen to what he had to say with regard to the affair. She determined that swallowing her pride and facing Jalen was well worth it if it was going to rid her life of Nina and the madness she brought. She also was going to have to take a trip to the other side of town and pay Nina a visit at her job at the strip club. She hated going into places like that, but desperate times called for desperate measures.

First thing first, she needed to call Jalen.

Rene dialed him up. "Hey. You busy? Can you talk?"

"What's up, Rene? I'm not busy. Just got to the office. You okay?"

"Not really. Um, do you think you can come over today? No rush, but I have a few things I need to discuss with you."

"Depends. What do you want to talk about? 'Cause I really don't have the energy to fight with you. I've had a very long week, and I really just want to keep my energy on the positive side."

"Fair enough. I totally get that. I do need to talk to you about some serious issues, but let's say we compromise. I will make sure that after we are done talking, there is a cold beer, some of my nachos, and a remote control waiting for you. How does that sound? Deal?"

"Ohhh, hell yeah! That sounds like a deal. A cold beer and your nachos? Yeah, I'm over there for sure! You can talk about whatever you need to. What time should I be there?"

"You are so silly. Come around four, four thirty."

"Bet! Do you need me to bring anything?"

"No, I have everything here."

"Cool. See you then."

Once Rene got herself and the kids dressed, she went downstairs to straighten up the house. She didn't want Jalen to think that the kids were living in filth since he had left.

The kids wanted to go outside and play, but with the possibility of Nina going ziggity-boom at any time, Rene didn't want to chance it. She told them they could play outside in the backyard if they agreed to take Jacob with them in his stroller in exchange for a Popsicle and a bag of fruit snacks. The kids were excited and agreed.

After Rene was done cleaning the house, she cut up the lettuce, tomatoes, and onions that she was going to need for the nachos. She also made sure to put a few beers in the freezer for Jalen. She prepared the meat and had everything ready on time.

Rene heard the doorbell ring and looked up at the clock on the microwave. It said 4:18. She knew that meant that Jalen was at the door.

"Kids! Go open the door for me," Rene shouted outside.

"Daddy!" yelled the children as they raced straight to the door, pushing Jacob in his stroller.

When they opened it, Jalen greeted them both with a huge hug and kiss and some goodies he'd stopped at the store and grabbed. They played and wrestled around for a bit, and then Jalen walked into the living room where Rene and Jacob were waiting.

"Smells good in here. Where's my plate?" Jalen asked jokingly.

"Nope. Sit down and talk first, eat later," Rene replied.

Jalen sat down on the couch. "Woooow! You set me up?" Jalen continued to joke.

Rene laughed. "No, I'm just smarter than the average bear. As soon as you eat those nachos and have a couple of beers, your conversation skills will not be as sharp as I need them to be," she explained.

"Very true! You always were smart," Jalen said, laughing. "So, what's up? Let's talk."

Rene let out a deep breath and proceeded to tell Jalen about everything that had been going on, including the incident the night before at the restaurant with Tyrese and his car. She could tell that Jalen was becoming agitated listening to her tell him how she had been out to eat with another man, but he didn't say a word at first. He just sat there with his eyes glued to the floor. Once she was done, she waited for Jalen to respond.

"Are you going to say anything?" Rene asked Jalen.

"What did you expect to get out of this dinner you had with Tyrese? Or were you on a date with him?" Jalen inquired.

"I wasn't expecting anything. It wasn't a date. It was two associates having dinner," Rene quickly answered. "I was just getting out of the house. He offered and I accepted."

Jalen wasn't buying it. "I'm not an idiot, Rene. You and that dude kickin' it now?"

"No! It was just dinner. After Nina came and showed her ass, it wasn't a very good one."

Jalen paused for a minute. It was obvious he was upset about the situation, but he didn't want Rene to see how much. He sat with his hand on his chin, slightly covering his mouth, not saying a word for a few minutes. Rene could see that he was biting his lip, which was what he did when he was angry but couldn't react.

"Well, I hope you have been putting two and two together," Jalen finally responded.

"What do you mean?" questioned Rene.

Jalen looked at Rene with a "don't be stupid" look. "I think it's plain to see that she has been following you. That's how she knew we were outside talking that day."

Rene gave a brief pause. "Following me? How do you know she wasn't following you? You are the one she thought she was going to spend the rest of her life with."

Jalen shook his head in frustration. "The only time she bothers me is before or after I'm around you. That's how she knew to send me that text that day. That's why she called you right before you went into the restaurant. That's how she knew you were there," Jalen tried to convince Rene.

After Rene gave it some thought, the bluntness of reality hit her like a ton of bricks. "You are absolutely right. Why didn't I think of that? Nina is stalking me and is completely out of control!"

"What are you going to do? What's on your mind?" Jalen inquired.

"I have an idea to get her to go away, but it won't work without you," answered Rene.

"Without me?" Jalen asked. "This should be interesting. Okay, I'm listening."

Rene explained, "I'm going to call her and say I need her to sign over her rights to Jacob and sign an order to allow paternity to be determined. I'll let her know that you and I have decided to work things out and we need this done in order to move on. There is a chance she may call you to see if this is true."

"I don't have a problem with that. I told you before, I'm not his father, and I will take a million tests to prove it," said Jalen. "I care about Jacob, but not as a father, more like an uncle. Come to think of it, why does this have to be some made-up story? Why can't it be the truth? If I prove to you that I'm not that baby's father, why can't we still work on us?" Jalen requested.

"Well, let me finish. You probably don't want to hear this, but when I was telling Tyrese about the fight and what you said really happened, he confirmed that one of the places the investigator saw you and Nina coming out of was a pool hall or whatever with a poker room in the basement."

"See? I told you!" yelled Jalen. "Damn. I guess I could have told you the same thing to prove it, huh?"

"Exactly! So, don't get too excited. That doesn't prove that you didn't sleep with her. It just proves that you had a gambling problem and didn't tell me. But if you are willing to take a test to prove he's not yours, I'm willing to maybe try to move forward," Rene agreed.

Jalen grabbed Rene's hand. "I kept the gambling thing from you, and I'm sorry. I regret it every day. I should have come to you when it started getting bad, but I was so ashamed. I was raised way better than that. I knew better than to put my family's well-being in jeopardy. I didn't want to disappoint you."

"You know I understand the power of addiction, Jay. Just like your job is to protect me, my job is to cover you when you're weak. Do you know about the power of the lioness?" Rene asked.

"I can't say that I do."

"In a pride, the lioness of the alpha lion watches over the pride when he goes out to hunt. She takes care of her cubs and looks out for danger to ensure the safety of the other lions. If the alpha lion gets wounded or becomes sick, she literally lays her body on top of his to protect him from other lions' attacks and allow him to heal. When he is strong again, she goes right back into her role of nurturing and supporting."

"Wow. I didn't know that. That is a beautiful thing," Jalen replied, astonished by what Rene shared.

"I'm your lioness, Jay. I know how to be submissive and let my man be the man he is. However, I'm also a boss and a very strong woman. I'm capable of taking care of this family in whatever way it needs to be taken care of if ever you can't. All of this could have been avoided had you remembered that. One thing we will definitely have issues with is me being able to trust you, especially if you don't trust me," Rene said, slowly sliding her hand onto Jalen's.

"You're right," Jalen agreed. "I wasn't thinking. I take full responsibility for that. Please know that I will do whatever it takes to build that trust back up. You and our kids are the most important things in the world to me. I'll never put our family in this predicament again," Jalen assured Rene.

Rene let a little smile slip out. "I know. I know." Jalen leaned in to kiss Rene, and she quickly moved, dodging his lips.

"Too soon?" Jalen asked.

"I would have to say yes. Definitely too soon," Rene responded.

Rene got up and went into the kitchen. She fixed Jalen a plate of nachos with the works: ground beef, ground turkey, shredded cheese, cheese sauce, lettuce, tomatoes, sour cream, and salsa. She grabbed him a beer from the freezer and set the others in the fridge. After grabbing a couple of pieces of paper towel, she walked back into the living room.

"A deal is a deal," Rene said as she handed Jalen the plate.

He quickly reached for it. "This looks so good! I am about to smash! Thanks so much, Rene," Jalen said, grinning from ear to ear.

Rene went and grabbed the remote control off of the entertainment system and handed it to Jalen. "You're welcome. Here is the last thing I promised you."

Jalen smiled, kissed her hand, and turned the TV to a college football game. It felt good to be home. It almost made Jalen feel like things were back to normal.

Once the game ended, Jalen decided it was best if he went ahead and left before Rene asked him to. Even though the day went great and he and Rene were getting along, he didn't want to push too hard and come on too strong. Jalen knew his wife. The couple reuniting was going to have to be slow and organic. More importantly, on Rene's terms.

The strong scent of cognac and weed quickly filled Rene's nose as she entered the Little Cuties Gentlemen's club. It took her just a couple of hours of lurking on some of the Facebook pages of people from the old neighborhood for her to figure out the name of Bruno's recently opened strip club. That was all she needed to return the favor of popping up unexpectedly to Nina. Rene paid the $20 admission fee, was checked with a handheld metal detector, and then walked through the next set of doors.

Ass, titties, and more ass and titties were all Rene could see at first glance through the black and flashing neon lights. Some of the women were gorgeous, others not so much, but they all had beautiful bodies and a lot of talent.

The main dancer on the stage looked like she might have been raised in a circus by acrobats. She scaled the twenty-foot metal pole up to the very top with lightning speed. She turned upside down, wrapped her legs around the pole, and slowly came back down, turning in a circle. When she was halfway down, she flipped right-side up, dropped down to the stage in a split, and twerked on the stage almost immediately. The men who surrounded the stage began to cheer and clap like crazy, tossing hundreds of dollars her way.

Damn! Impressive! That was amazing! I wonder if she went to some type of school to learn how to do that, Rene thought.

She looked around and found an empty seat at the bar. She quickly went and claimed it and called the bartender over.

"Hello, there. How can I help you, honey?" asked the cute and bright-eyed bartender.

"Hello. Can I have a shot of Patrón on ice with a lemon please?" ordered Rene.

"You sure can. Is that all you need?" said the waitress as she began to pour Rene's drink.

"Actually, I do need one more thing. Do you know if Nina is working right now?" inquired Rene.

"Nina? I don't think we have a Nina. Is she a dancer?" said the bartender.

Rene was confused. She knew that she had come to the right place, so her first thought was that, once again, Nina lied about what she was doing, and Rene had just wasted her time and gas driving to the other side of the city to pop up on her. After a little thought, Rene remembered that in the club world, no one knew Nina's real name. They all called her NiNi.

"I'm sorry, I meant NiNi. Do you know if NiNi is working?" Rene corrected herself.

"Oh! Yeah, she's here. She's in the back office. Did you need me to go get her?" offered the bartender.

"If you could, that would be so lovely of you. When you get back, pour you a shot on me," Rene said as she set $40 on the bar.

"Thank you! My drink is only ten dollars. The total tab for both of our drinks is only twenty-five dollars," the bartender informed Rene.

"That's cool. Keep the change." Rene winked and smiled.

"Okay. I appreciate that. Let me go get NiNi for you." The bartender grabbed the money off the bar, cashed Rene out, and put the remaining change in her tip jar. She then disappeared down a hallway to the right of the bar.

Rene sat there patiently, sipping her drink, listening to the music, and continuing to be amazed by the acrobatic abilities of the strippers. She suddenly heard a familiar voice.

"Rene? What the fuck are you doing here?" questioned Nina.

"Surprise! I can do the pop-up shit too," replied Rene sarcastically.

Nina gave Rene a blank stare.

"I need to talk, and I want to talk now," demanded Rene.

"Okay. Follow me," Nina answered.

Rene threw the rest of her drink back, grabbed her phone and wallet, and proceeded to follow Nina down the same hallway the bartender had walked down. Once they reached the end of the hallway, Nina stopped walking and leaned back against the wall.

"Why would you come here?" Nina asked. "This isn't a place for you. You don't belong here."

"Girl, shut up!" Rene was obviously irritated. "You are not my mama. I can go wherever the fuck I want to."

Nina was shocked at Rene's response. "I wasn't trying to be your mama. I was just trying to look out for your well-being."

"I'm good," Rene boldly stated.

"How have you been? You look really good. It's so good to see you up close and personal, and to hear your voice, too. I missed you so much!" Nina shared.

Rene squinted in confusion at Nina. "Are you fucking nuts? This is not a 'kiss and make up' situation, dum-dum. This is not a 'forgive and forget' visit. I still don't fuck with you. You're still on my shit list. Especially after the bullshit you pulled the other night. Who the fuck does silly stuff like that?"

"I'm sorry about that," Nina apologized. "I had been smoking and drinking and I just lost my cool. I just wanted to see you."

"That was way beyond losing your cool, so per usual, save that shit. I don't care, so don't waste either of our time trying to explain anything. I'm here right now because I need you to do something," clarified Rene. "And I need you to do it right away."

"Okay. What is it? I got you. Whatever you need," Nina responded anxiously.

"I need you to sign over your rights to Jacob and agree to let Jalen take a paternity test," Rene said with a straight face.

"Wh . . . what? Why do you want me to do that?" Nina asked in a faint voice as if someone had knocked the wind out of her. "You really just going to take my baby from me, Rene?"

"I'm not taking anything from you. I'm doing what's best for my godson and my marriage. Jalen and I are trying to work it out. In order for us to move on, I need to know if Jacob is really his son," Rene expounded.

"Don't you believe me?" Nina questioned.

"Uhhh, no! I don't. I thought I made that very clear when I put you out of my house. Then again, I can't say I really believe Jalen either. That's why I want the test," answered Rene. "I want to go into this healing process with my eyes wide open and all questions answered. I need all mess and bullshit to go away."

"Even if the test says that Jacob is not his, that doesn't mean he wasn't sleeping with me," Nina revealed.

"You are really brave to say that shit dead to my face like that. It's taking all I have not to knock your freakin' face off right now!" Rene informed Nina. "You're right. It doesn't prove you weren't being a whore and he wasn't being a weak-minded, no-good man. However, it will be enough for me to move on. Jalen is a man. When it comes to pussy, men do stupid shit. I can forgive him for that. That's neither here nor there. Will you do it?" Rene asked again.

Nina was silent. Rene looked at her, waiting for a response, but it was like Nina had mentally left the building. Her body was there, but her eyes said her thoughts were in another time and place. Rene starting snapping her fingers in Nina's face, yelling hello over and over. Nina finally snapped back.

"Ye . . . yeah. I hear you," confirmed Nina. "Are you willing to forgive me? Like you are Jalen?"

"I can't answer that. I'm still too angry. What I can say is even if I do find the strength to forgive you, we will never be friends again. I don't trust you. You burned and destroyed the bridge of our sisterhood."

"Wow. So regardless of whatever I say, whatever I do, I can forget about us ever being back to the way we were? I don't get that. How can you forgive Jalen but you can't forgive me?" Nina asked.

"Jalen is my husband!" Rene said passionately. "I made a lifetime commitment to him. I'm in a forever covenant between God, Jalen, and me. He is the father of my children. I owe it to my kids to try to fix my marriage. Yes, you were my friend, but I don't have those type of ties or obligations to you. I gave you no reason to do what you did to me. I don't owe you anything. You can't compare yourself to Jalen. That's like comparing apples to oranges."

Nina was devastated. Rene's words crushed her down to the pit of her soul.

"I understand. It really hurts to hear you say that, but I get it. Don't worry. It will all work out. If you want me out of your life forever, then I'll give that to you," Nina said in a bitter but sad tone.

"Okay good," replied Rene. "Oh, one more thing. Know that I'm petitioning to get a PPO on you. If you and your hood-rat, dick-sucking, bad-weave-wearing, fugly-looking, trick-ass friends keep playing on my phone or come anywhere near me or my kids, you will go to jail or I will shoot you. Those are your only two options."

Rene didn't give Nina a chance to respond. She turned to exit the hallway, but Nina grabbed her arm. "Don't leave," yelled Nina. "Can't you just stay a little longer? It's been so long since we've kicked it and had a good time together."

Rene snatched her arm away and pushed Nina against the wall really hard. "Bitch, get your hands off of me!" demanded Rene. "I will beat yo' ass ten times worse than I did the last time if you ever touch me again!"

At that moment Rene heard a door open, and she quickly looked to her right. Bruno, Jody, and a dancer were standing in the doorway. Bruno had a blunt hanging off his lip.

"Everything all right out here, ladies?" he asked, looking at Nina.

"Everything is fine, Bruno. You can go back in the office," answered Nina.

"You sure?" Jody questioned. "What's up, Rene?" Jody gave Rene a dirty look.

Rene gave her one right back.

"Rene! I thought you looked familiar. This is the forever friend, right? Long time no see, sweetheart. Wait, did you come looking to be a dancer? With an ass like that, I know we could make some good money together," said Bruno. "We can go into my office right now, and you can audition."

"Nigga, please. Do I look like I would ever take my clothes off for money? You got me confused with this trick right here." Rene pointed to Nina. "Believe me, if I did want to degrade myself in front of a bunch of drunken fools, it wouldn't be in no ghetto-ass, run-down shit hole like this!" Rene snapped. "And what was that 'what's up, Rene,' Jody? Don't come for me. I know you might have all the punk-ass little dicks scared, but not me. Is there something you wanna say?"

"What did you say, bitch?" Bruno asked angrily. "Do you know who you're talking to? I'm not a lie-down type of guy."

"Please give me a reason. I've been wanting to beat your ass for a minute now."

"Bruno, that's enough! I said everything is cool. I got it," Nina interrupted. "You too, Jody. I got it. Just go back in the office please. I'll be in there in a minute."

Bruno and Jody did not budge. They did not like Rene, and they were not going to give her an opportunity to beat Nina up again.

"I don't have time for this shit," Rene blurted out before turning to face Nina. "The probate court opens at eight thirty in the morning. Let me know when you file that paper. Do not call or text me unless it's to say it has been handled. I mean that shit!" Rene instructed Nina, pointing her finger in her face.

Rene left the hallway while Nina, Bruno, Jody, and the dancer watched her walk away. She could not get to her car fast enough. When she peeled out of the parking lot, she felt so empowered, as if she could finally take a deep breath without choking. Rene was finally regaining control of her life. She was starting to see a little light at the end of the tunnel.

Rene prayed that the final chapter to the madness would be coming soon and all the headaches and stress would be over. After Nina signed the papers, she could move on with her life and allow Rene and Jalen to do the same.

A few weeks passed, and there was no word from Nina. No texts, anonymous phone calls, pop-up visits, or anything. However, Rene had spoken to Tyrese. She shared with him what took place at the strip club and her conversation with Jalen. Tyrese assured Rene that he would not interfere with her trying to work on her marriage. He had a strong respect for the sanctity of marriage and would never want to be the reason one failed. He also let her know that if the test came back and said that Jalen was not the father, then he would be willing to take one to see if Jacob was his son. Tyrese vowed to take care of Jacob if he was indeed the father. He would never let a child with his blood flowing through his or her veins go without.

The curtain had closed, the audience was clapping, and the drama had ended . . . so Rene thought.

Rene was in the office working on her Saturday for the month. She actually didn't mind. With all of the chaos happening in her life, she arrived to work late or left early. She had fallen a little behind in her work, and she needed to get caught up. There were only four other people in the office, which allowed Rene to work uninterrupted. She planned on staying in the office for as long as it took to finish. There were zero plans for the evening on her agenda, and the kids were spending the weekend with her mom. Rene's niece and nephew were visiting from out of town, and her mom wanted all the kids to spend the weekend together. Rene didn't mind, but she hated being home alone, so there was no reason to rush home from work.

Nina never did file the paperwork to release her rights. Rene wasn't surprised. Nina was as flaky as they came, and her not doing what she said she would was nothing new. Jalen, however, moved forward with getting a DNA test. The results had not come back yet, so Rene insisted that he continue to live with his cousin.

When Rene arrived at her office early that Saturday, she hoped that her work would keep her mind occupied and allow her not to feel anxious. Even though everything seemed to have simmered down, Rene just had a strange feeling in her gut. She couldn't pinpoint exactly what was going on.

She worked through the day. At 7:28 p.m., according to her computer, she had officially been at work for nine and a half hours, and it was time to shut it down and head home. Rene was mentally drained, and she had a weird feeling in her gut. Being that she had not eaten since noon, she attributed the feeling to hunger and brushed it off. As she was packing up to leave, she noticed she had missed several calls from Jalen and one of her neighbors.

Why is Jalen blowing me up all of a sudden? And what does Heather want? I'll call them both back after I get settled at home and put some food in my belly. I'm hangry right now and not in the mood to talk.

Rene stopped at her favorite Chinese restaurant and ordered a shrimp egg foo young combination platter with shrimp fried rice. She then stopped at the specialty store and grabbed a bottle of wine and her favorite dessert, lemon chiffon cake.

As Rene turned into her subdivision, she noticed a bunch of people and flashing lights close to her house. Not just any flashing lights, but police and ambulance lights. Once she was on her block, she could see that the emergency vehicles were actually at her house.

"What in the world is going on now?" she said as she pulled up. She took off her seat belt and quickly ran to the front of the crowd that had gathered. As she was fighting through the crowd, she heard Jalen call out her name.

"Jalen! This is nuts! What are you doing here? Do you know what's going on?" Rene anxiously questioned. "Why are they at the house?"

"Heather and her husband gave me a call on my cell. You never took my name off the contact list in the neighborhood directory. They were trying to get a hold of you!" Jalen said in a very excited tone.

"I know. I was at work, and I saw the calls as I was leaving. I was going to call you back when I got home. What is going on?" Rene yelled. Her anxiousness was turning into fear, and she needed Jalen to tell her what was happening.

"I don't know how to tell you this, but . . ." Jalen stuttered.

"Just spit it out already," demanded Rene.

"Nina—"

Rene swiftly interrupted. "Oh, Lord! What has this cuckoo bird done now? I'm going to kill her with my bare hands if she did something to my house!"

Rene became so angry she took off running toward her house to see what damage Nina had inflicted this time. Once she reached the end of her driveway, she saw a white sheet covering what appeared to be the body of a human in her driveway. There was blood everywhere. Rene screamed from the shock. She did not realize that Jalen was right behind her.

Jalen grabbed Rene around the waist to keep her from falling down.

"That's what I was trying to tell you," Jalen said, out of breath from chasing Rene. "Nina is dead. She came to the house, and I guess because you weren't here, she sat in the driveway and slit her wrists. The police said they found an empty pill bottle of oxycodone in her pocket. By the time anyone realized what was going on, it was too late. She was already gone."

Rene's heart dropped down to the bottom of her feet. Her knees buckled and Jalen had to continue to hold her up and keep her from falling. She could not believe what was happening. As much as Nina had put her through, she would never wish death on her, or on anyone for that matter. If she had known that Nina was this unstable, she would have tried to find her some help. She would have listened to her and made sure she didn't hurt herself.

Rene thought back to all the times that Nina tried to reach out to her and how she never wanted anything to do with her. Rene was always quick to turn her back on Nina.

Rene laid her head on Jalen's chest and continued to sob. "I didn't know! Oh God, I promise I didn't know!" were the only words that Rene could seem to gather up and say out loud.

Jalen's heart hurt so badly for Rene. He had never seen her so distraught. He walked her to his truck and helped her in. He parked Rene's car in front of the neighbors' house and let them know what was going on. Jalen didn't think it was a good idea for Rene to stay at the house, especially alone, so he drove her to her mother's. He called Ms. Martha and let her know that they were on the way. Rene was shaking uncontrollably.

When they arrived at Ms. Martha's house, Jalen sat her on the couch and just held her. Ms. Martha already had some tea ready for her. She put the kids to bed so that they would not bother Rene.

The guilt that was slowly stacking up on Rene's heart was heavy. Why didn't she see the signs? Why would Nina do something like this? It all was so heavy on her heart and hard to comprehend. Rene eventually fell asleep in Jalen's arms on her mother's couch.

The next morning, Rene's mom and Jalen were in the kitchen, trying to figure out how they should proceed. Jalen knew that Rene was going to be a wreck, and they had to figure out how they were going to tell the kids.

"My poor, poor child," Ms. Martha repeated, slightly rocking in her chair. "I hate that this happened. I was never a fan of Nina's but never wanted any hurt or harm to come to her.

"It still seems so unreal," Jalen added. "When Rene saw Nina's body lying in the driveway, the scream that she let out sent chills down my spine. She was an emotional disaster after that. Do you think she'll be open to staying here with you for a few days?" Jalen asked.

"Why can't she stay at home with you?" Ms. Martha rebutted.

"I would love that!" Jalen quickly replied. "I'm not sure if Rene is ready for that. I don't want to seem like I'm using this tragedy to wriggle my way back home."

"I guess you're right," Ms. Martha agreed. "Whatever she decides to do, I will be here for her."

As the two were getting a game plan together, there was a knock at the door.

"Who on earth could that be?" questioned Ms. Martha.

"I don't know. I'll go check for you," Jalen said as he walked toward the front door.

When Jalen reached the door, he could see that it was one of the detectives from the night before. After they'd given statements last night, he'd told the cops Rene's mom's address and phone number just in case they needed anything before Jalen and Rene returned. He assumed the detectives must have gotten it from them. When Jalen opened the door, he could tell by the look on the detective's face that something wasn't right.

"Detective?" said Jalen. "How can I help you?"

"Good morning. My name is Detective O'Neil. I'm sorry to disturb you and your family so early, but I have something that I thought you might want to see."

"Really? What might that be?" asked Jalen.

"Lying on the front seat of Nina's car was an envelope with a letter inside. It was addressed to your wife. I thought she might want to read it. So, I made a copy of it," described Detective O'Neil. He handed Jalen an envelope. Jalen pulled out the letter and unfolded it. He could not believe what he was looking at. It was the letter that Nina had written to Rene before she committed suicide.

"What are all these dark spots?" Jalen asked, examining the copied letter.

"Well, it's blood."

Jalen wasn't expecting that answer and was a little shocked by the response.

Detective O'Neal continued, "I know it's a lot to take in right now. However, this letter should resolve a lot of the issues you and your wife are having. That's another reason why I really wanted her to have it."

"I'll make sure she gets it. Thank you for bringing it to her," said Jalen.

"No problem. No problem at all. Just doing my job. If you or your wife have any questions, please give me a call," responded Detective O'Neil. He handed Jalen one of his cards.

When Jalen walked back into the kitchen, Rene was awake. She was sitting at the island, drinking some more tea that her mother had made her.

"Who was that?" Rene asked him.

"That was one of the detectives who's handling Nina's case. Detective O'Neil is his name." Jalen hesitated. "He had something for you. Something he thought you would want to see."

"What? Something for me?" Rene asked.

"Before I give you this, I need to know how you are doing. Emotionally," said Jalen. "You sure you can handle this?"

"I mean, of course I'm sad and upset, but I'm okay. The initial shock as passed. I'm okay. Why? What is it? What did he bring to me?" questioned Rene.

"It's Nina's suicide letter," answered Jalen.

Ms. Martha gasped. "My God!" she cried out.

Rene was a little stunned at first, but a part of her needed to read that letter. She needed to know what was going through Nina's head and why she did what she did.

"I'm okay, Jalen. Just give me the letter," said Rene.

Jalen handed the letter to Rene, then sat down at the table with Ms. Martha. When Rene opened the letter, she realized that the dark spots all over the Xeroxed letter were Nina's blood and tears. She didn't even have to ask. She walked into the living room. She wanted to read the letter in private.

Dear Rene,

If you are reading this letter, then it means that I have given in to the pain I have battled with for years. I have left this earth by my own hands. I'm sorry you had to see me like this, but my dying desire was to take my last breath as close to you as possible. There are a lot of things about me that you didn't know, and I think I owe it to you to finally come clean and tell you the entire truth.

I want to first say that Jacob is not Jalen's baby. Tyrese is without a doubt his father. I know seeing these words probably intensifies your hate for me due to all the turmoil I caused, but it was for a good reason.

Jalen's version of the story about the night in the city is true. I did bump into him and his boys. Jalen wasn't cheating, but he wasn't acting like a married man either. Everything I did that night was to simply test Jalen. To show you that he was a liar and a jerk. It didn't work. I blamed it on being drunk. He said he was cool, but I guess that wasn't really the case.

A short time after that happened, I started to hear his name in conversations among some bottle girls and waitresses. They were saying that he was acting like he was some big baller and ladies' man. When I saw him while I was waitressing at the pool hall, I knew that you didn't know he was there. I confronted him, and he begged me not to say anything. I agreed, but from that point on, I knew he couldn't be trusted. I knew the rumors were actually true.

I pretended to be his friend and use some of my connections to get him access to all of the hot poker spots. He was so hooked on gambling it wasn't hard to do. When he would start drinking, he also would start to get real touchy-feely with some of the waitresses and bar sluts who were always floating around the room. I just knew in my gut that he either had cheated or would cheat on you. I never was able to catch Jalen doing anything. When Tyrese showed me those pictures, I figured if I told him his hunch was right, he would tell you and reveal Jalen's secrets. At first, Tyrese never said a word. Instead he kept it to himself all that time.

By now I guess you are wondering why I went through all of this. The truth is, I'm in love with you, Rene. I have been since we were teenagers. I know how you feel about that, which is why I never told you I was bisexual. Tyrese did know. We even talked about having threesomes when we got married. I'm guessing he never shared that with you either. A lot of the chicks I used to introduce you to weren't just my homegirls. They were also my lovers, or they were strippers that Jody and I were managing. That's how I was always able to keep money during the majority of my pregnancy.

Jalen is no good for you and not good enough for you. He doesn't appreciate your beauty or your dedication to your family. He took advantage of your love and loyalty for him. He lied about his business being in trouble just so he could go out and gamble. I would have never done that to you. I would have always been there for you and shown you the love you deserve every single day. The day you kicked my ass and put me out, I was hoping that you would believe me and see that I loved you and not Jalen. I wanted to get him out of the way so that you and I could raise our kids together as a family. My plan backfired on me horribly. Instead, you cut me out of your life and didn't want anything to do with me. I lost it. I panicked.

I did all of those crazy things after I moved out because I was confused and desperate. You wouldn't even talk to me, and I was starting to feel like I was drowning. I didn't know what else to do. I thought if I harassed Jalen and Tyrese enough, they would leave you alone. You would get lonely and come back to me. That didn't work either. It only intensified your hate toward me. The thought of you dealing with pain because of me and us never being friends again were things I could not live with. My whole world revolved around you. You were my rock. You always loved me in spite of my craziness. Never judged me for anything I did.

You are the definition of beauty, inside and out. There were so many times that I just wanted to grab you and kiss you and tell you how I felt. I knew that wasn't going to fly with you. Now that you're officially out of my life, I have no reason to live. Please do me one last favor. Please take care of my baby, and remember that no matter what people tell you, I loved you and it was real! Please find it in your heart to forgive me for everything I've done, including taking my life.

Love Forever,
Nina

Tears were streaming down Rene's face, one by one onto the Luther Vandross T-shirt her mother had given her to sleep in. All of the chaos that had transpired over the last six months and taken its toll on the lives of all parties involved stemmed from lies that were created by one disturbed individual.

"Nina was in love with me?" Rene said to herself. "How did I not see that?"

Rene began to blame herself for everything that had taken place. Putting Jalen out, Jalen's and Tyrese's cars being destroyed, the prank calls and text messages, the incident at the restaurant, and now Nina's death were all results of Rene not seeing what was right in her face.

She walked into the kitchen and gave the letter to Jalen. He began to read it, and the farther down the page he read, the bigger his eyes got.

"This is unreal!" stated Jalen in total shock.

Rene started to blurt out an apology. "I'm sorry for not trusting you. I'm sorry for pushing you away. I didn't know she felt that way. I'm so sorry, Jay. I wish I could take it all back."

Jalen grabbed his wife and held her as tight as he could. He whispered in her ear, "Stop it! None of this is your fault. You're not psychic. How could you have known what was in Nina's head or how things would end? If anything, I should be the one apologizing. If I had just told you about the night of the bachelor party and that I was struggling with a gambling addiction, Nina would not have had a reason to feel the way she felt. That is something that I own and regret. It's hard to see right now, but everything is going to be okay. Please know that, baby! I need you not to worry. There is nothing for you to be sorry about. She had us all fooled, not just you."

Chapter 11

Life Goes On

The next few weeks were beyond difficult for Rene and her entire family. She and Jalen were burdened with the task of explaining to the kids what had happened to their aunt NiNi. Although the police made the official notification to Nina's mom and her sisters, Rene still felt like she should reach out to them as well.

"Hello," said a familiar voice over the phone.

"Hi, Ms. Nichelle. It's Rene."

"Rene! Wow, what a surprise. I didn't expect to hear from you. It's been a long time," Nichelle said loudly.

"Yes, it has. I wish that I were calling under better circumstances. I wanted to touch base with you. Let you know that I am here if you need help with any of the arrangements for Nina."

"What do you mean?" asked Nichelle.

Her question caused Rene's eyebrow to raise. She didn't understand why Nichelle would ask that. "Oh, well, the police did contact you, didn't they?" Rene inquired.

"About Nina?" Nichelle responded. "Yeah, they did. I'm trying to figure out why you called saying you would help me. I was about to call you and your mom and offer my help to you."

"Pardon me?" Rene stated. "I am lost. Help me? Help me do what?"

"Look at here. Nina decided a long time ago that you and your family were more important than her own mother. When she kidnapped my kids and helped my mama and daddy get custody of them, we stopped being family. I just assumed you and your people would take care of her funeral. She's not my responsibility."

Rene was speechless and saddened by what Nichelle was saying. Once she became addicted to drugs, she stopped being much of a mother to Nina and her sisters. Now that Nichelle had been clean for a couple of years, she still was not being a good mother to Nina.

"Ms. Nichelle, how can you say that? Nina was a kid when she did what she did. She was just trying to do what was best for her sisters. You were really sick back then."

"Bitch, I know what I was!" yelled Nichelle.

"Please calm down. I wasn't trying to be disrespectful or rude," Rene assured her.

"You know, you and yo' mama have always thought y'all was better than me. You think I don't know how strung out I was? I don't need your boogie, stuck-up ass to remind me of that! I'm clean now, and that's all that matters," said Nichelle.

A warm ball of anger was slowly growing in the pit of Rene's gut. It was one thing to throw insults at her, but to start throwing them at Ms. Marsha was crossing the line.

"If not giving your kid away to your drug dealer to pay off a debt you owe him makes my mother stuck-up, then goddamn it, I guess she's stuck-up! Not to mention all of the food, clothes, and rides she gave to your kid over the years, never asking you for a thing in return!"

"What? Do you want me to give her a gold star or something? I never asked her to do any of that shit," Nichelle rebutted.

"You have a lot of fucking nerve, lady. When you were out in alleys sucking dick for money, Nina was working her ass off to make sure your kids didn't go hungry and that they had lights and heat when they got home from school," Rene reminded her. "Even though you disowned Nina, she never disowned you. Even after all of the fucked-up things you put her through, she still loved you. I know for a fact you never returned a dollar she sent you over the years, so save that betrayal shit. If you were that upset, you wouldn't have accepted a dime from her. You know what? I'm glad you're sober. That means it's not the drugs making you act like an evil, bottom-of-the-barrel, bitter bitch of a woman. It's clearly just who and what you are! Don't worry about Nina's funeral or your grandson, Jacob, whom you have not asked about even once! I'll take care of the funeral, and I'll take care of Jacob. Have a miserable life, Ms. Nichelle. You deserve it!" Rene wished. She pushed the end button on her phone and threw it down next to her on the couch. When she looked up, Jalen was standing in the entryway staring at her.

"You okay?" asked Jalen.

"I guess. I really don't know," answered Rene.

"Who was that on the phone?"

"Nina's mom, Nichelle. Do you know she had the audacity to take jabs at me and my mom? She even brought up Nina 'kidnapping' her kids and helping her parents get custody."

Jalen looked puzzled. "Wasn't she hooked on drugs really bad?"

"Yes!" Rene responded. "She told me she assumed that I was taking care of Nina's funeral because Nina loved me and my mother more than her. What kind of mother thinks like that?"

Jalen shook his head in disbelief. He walked over to the couch and sat down next to Rene. "That shit is sad," expressed Jalen. "What are you going to do?"

"What I've done for the last twenty years. What I always do. I'm going to take care of my friend," said Rene with one tear rolling down her cheek.

Once again, the only person to have Nina's back was Rene. However, it turned out that Nina wasn't as stupid and ghetto as she had let on, and ultimately, she had her own back.

Apparently, with the money she was earning from all of her hustles and men over the years, Nina had established a pretty nice balance in her bank account: $185, 632 to be exact. She also was paying a monthly premium for some top-of-the-line life insurance policy that was not affected by her committing suicide.

When Nina's father died, her family went through hell trying to get his business in order. He didn't have any life insurance at all. Family and friends who said they would help her mom pay for the funeral, Nina found out later, asked for their money back or wanted her mom to sleep with them. It was a hot mess, to say the least.

Nina didn't want to leave her son in that same predicament if ever something were to happen to her. She was not in denial about the lifestyle she lived, and she knew she had to make sure that the money would be paid out to take care of him regardless of the manner of her death. To ensure this would happen, she'd consulted with an attorney who helped her select a life insurance plan and develop a will.

The details of her will and life insurance policy left everything to Rene and Jacob. The total payout of the policy was $250,000. $15,000 was to go toward Nina's funeral arrangements. $100,000 was to be put in a trust for Jacob. He would receive four payments on his birthday at the ages of 18, 25, 30, and 35. The remaining $135,000 all went to Rene.

It took a long time for Rene to be able to accept the money. She knew that Nina really wanted her to have it, but the pain, tears, and blood that were shed in order for her to receive it bothered Rene a lot. She wasn't able to deal with the reality that her dear friend took her own life because she thought that Rene didn't love her anymore.

Rene took a leave from work. She couldn't focus on tasks for too long and had developed generalized anxiety disorder. It was extremely hard for her to be alone without having a full-blown panic attack. Jalen had to rush Rene to the hospital on two different occasions because they didn't know what was wrong at first. She'd had nightmares for weeks after she saw Nina lying in her driveway with a white sheet draped over her. She could not get that image out of her head no matter how hard she tried.

To make the situation worse, Nina's family, especially her mother, was in an uproar when they found out that her funeral was completely paid for and that she actually left a lot of money in the bank and in her insurance policy.

Rene found herself being dragged in and out of court for months on top of months. Their first argument was that Nina and Rene weren't friends anymore when she died and Nina just forgot to change her will and beneficiaries on her policy and bank account. They even had Shanequa and Jody come and testify about all the craziness that took place leading up to Nina's suicide. Rene's lawyer countered their theory by providing the suicide note as evidence and testimony from Nina's attorney to prove that Nina still cared for Rene and wanted her to have the money.

Their second attempt to get the money was the absolute worst. Nichelle tried to fight Rene for custody of Jacob. It amazed Rene that when Nichelle thought

Nina was just a hustling stripper with no money or assets, she didn't want anything to do with the funeral or her grandson. She did not give Rene one nickel toward Nina's funeral and had the nerve to show up late. When Nichelle saw Jacob, she smiled at him, kissed him on the forehead, and kept it moving, not showing up at all to the repast. Now that there was a little money involved, Nichelle and Nina's sisters were all in court crying to a family court mediator about how much they loved Nina and wanted to make sure her son would be in their lives. They were selfish and greedy efforts that went in vain.

Their case never made it in front of a judge. In Nina's will, it clearly stated, "In the event of unforeseen sickness, or my untimely death, it is my preference and desire that my best friend and son's godmother, Rene Martin, have sole legal and physical custody of him."

The probate court had already proven that despite their recent falling out, it was clear that the details of the will were valid and still what Nina wanted to happen. Case dismissed.

Rene used her time off to start going to therapy and marriage counseling with Jalen. They put everything on the table and were working through their issues. Rene asked Jalen to move back in, and he eagerly obliged. They weren't at 100 percent but were really close to it. It took some time, but Rene was finally able to cope with the guilt weighing her down. Looking at Jacob's smile every day was helping her fight through it.

Nina's death created somewhat of a media frenzy. Strangers from different media outlets were constantly calling the house and Rene's and Jalen's cell phones, sending messages over Facebook, and trying to bombard them outside of their home. It was all just too much. The constant stares, glares, and whispers from nosy neighbors were the final straw. Even Jalen had his fill of everything and had run out patience. Rene and Jalen decided to put their house up for sale, pack up the kids, and move to a different city in the Detroit metro area to give their marriage and their family a fresh start.

A bright spot in the Martin household was that Jalen's landscaping business was booming like never before. Through some major networking and client referrals, he was able to secure big-time contracts with a few local celebrities and sports figures for their homes and businesses. After that, his business took off! Jalen opened up three more locations in Flint, Allen Park, and Livonia to better serve clients in those areas.

Rene was finally strong enough to go back to work, and it was business as usual. It was like she was never off. She picked up right where she left off, impressing the hell out of her boss and colleagues. Her boss was so pleased with her ability to bounce back and her work performance, he was 100 percent on board with letting her keep her schedule of three days in the office and two at home. Rene was very thankful for that. It kept her from getting burned out and feeling overwhelmed, and her anxiety was under control. It also ensured that she would be able to spend quality time with her kids and give the needed energy to rebuilding her marriage with Jalen.

A few months after Nina's funeral, Rene reached out to Tyrese. There was an important conversation about Nina's death and Jacob that needed to take place between the two of them. This time, Rene made sure that Jalen was okay with her meeting up with Tyrese. Of course, Jalen didn't like it, but he understood it was something that needed to happen. Tyrese agreed to meet Rene at a small Coney Island restaurant so that the two of them could talk.

When Tyrese arrived at the restaurant, he walked through the door and quickly found Rene sitting in a booth with two Detroit-style Coney dogs, one that was half eaten, an order of onion rings, and a Coke sitting in front of her. Tyrese smiled, somewhat impressed that a small woman like Rene could throw down on some food like that.

"I'm sorry, am I late?" asked Tyrese as he took his blazer off and slid into the booth to join Rene.

Rene smirked. She knew Tyrese was asking that because she had food and had started eating already. "No, sir. You are not late. You're actually a few minutes early," laughed Rene, checking the time on her phone. "I was starving! I came here straight from work, and I just couldn't wait for you to get here to eat."

Tyrese joined her in laughing. "I've definitely been there before," Tyrese empathized. "I get so busy at work that sometimes the day just gets away from me. Next thing I know it's four thirty, five o'clock, and all I've had to eat is a bagel and a cup of coffee."

"Exactly!" confirmed Rene. "That is what happened to me today. So, I'm not trying to be rude, but I also did not want to pass out due to having low blood sugar. It was in everyone's best interest that I get some food in my system ASAP," joked Rene as she took a big bite out of her Coney and shoved two onion rings in her mouth.

Tyrese's laugh grew in volume as he watched Rene pig out. The waitress came over and took his order. He followed Rene's lead and ordered a Coney, chili-cheese fries, and a Coke.

"How are you holding up? How's your family?" questioned Tyrese.

"We're making it," replied Rene. "Jalen and I are still trying to work out a few wrinkles but we're in a pretty good place. The kids are handling everything better than I am, to be honest. They were sad at first, but they've bounced back with no problem. Jacob is so big. He's walking now."

"That's all great to hear. I'm glad your family is solid and healthy," praised Tyrese.

"Yeah. I am too. It was really hard for a minute. I have something for you," Rene informed him.

She reached into her purse and pulled out a piece of paper. It was Nina's suicide letter. Rene handed it to Tyrese and asked him to read it.

It broke Tyrese's heart to read the words on the paper. He really cared about Nina and had no idea she felt that way.

"Whoa! That is a lot to take in! I hope this doesn't offend you," said Tyrese, "but this is some twisted shit!"

"No argument from me," agreed Rene. "I still sometimes can't believe that this wasn't a bad movie but my real life. I had nightmares about this for a long time."

"It doesn't really matter at this point, but I want you to know that I truly did love Nina. I loved her more than I have ever loved any woman in my life! I know we were complete opposites, but she did it for me. I would have taken really good care of her if she had let me," Tyrese shared.

"There is not a bone in my body that doubts that, Tyrese. I wish things could have ended differently, but they didn't. It does not change the fact that there is a handsome little boy who has lost his mother and doesn't know his father," stated Rene. "I know what I'm about to ask you is a huge, life-altering request, but I would really appreciate it if you could get a blood test to confirm you are Jacob's dad. If it comes back that you are, be in his life. He will always have Uncle Jalen, but he deserves to know his father."

"This isn't a big request at all," Tyrese replied. "It was on my mind to address with you anyway. Say no more, Rene. I give you my word that I'll take the test. Can you set it all up?"

"I most certainly can. I'll make an appointment at a lab I've worked with before and let you know when they need you to go."

"Perfect! Sounds like a plan," said Tyrese.

The waitress came and placed Tyrese's food down in front of him. He picked up his Coney and motioned for Rene to pick up hers too.

"To the truth and new beginnings." Tyrese lifted his Coney to Rene.

"The truth and new beginnings," repeated Nina.

"Cheers!" the two yelled out while tapping their Coneys together. They took a big bite together and shared a laugh.

The next day, Rene contacted the lab and set appointments for her to bring Jacob and for Tyrese to give DNA. She texted the info to Tyrese, and he responded saying he got the text and he would for sure make his appointment. Tyrese kept his word and took a paternity test. After an excruciating two-week wait, the results confirmed that Tyrese was indeed Jacob's father.

When the results first came back, Rene was a little worried that Tyrese would try to take Jacob from her. She was fully aware that as Jacob's biological father, Tyrese had the law on his side. It was well within his right to take custody of his son, and there would be nothing that Rene could do unless she could prove Tyrese was unfit.

Once paternity was confirmed, Tyrese met with both Jalen and Rene to discuss next steps. They brought Jacob with them. When Tyrese entered the door and saw Jacob sitting in his stroller, he was in awe at how perfect he was. He greeted Rene with a hug, formally introduced himself to Jalen, and they shook hands.

"I appreciate you guys coming here to meet me. I've been so nervous all day," Tyrese shared.

"About what?" questioned Rene after taking a sip of her coffee.

"Ummm, meeting my son," Tyrese answered, giving Rene a look that said, "Duh."

Jalen and Rene laughed.

"I know. I was just messing with you," joked Rene.

Jalen unstrapped Jacob from his stroller and handed him to Tyrese.

"Congratulations, my man," Jalen wished him. "It's a boy!"

Tyrese was grinning from ear to ear.

"Hey there, little guy. How are ya?" Tyrese greeted Jacob. Jacob cracked a smile at Tyrese, causing his eyes to fill with water. He managed to squeeze out, "He's perfect!" before he was completely choked up.

Rene's heart was fluttering watching Tyrese and Jacob enjoy each other. She started to think about Nina. If only she and Jalen had been honest from the beginning, they might be on a double date. Jacob would have both of his parents, and Tyrese would have a wife.

"I know that he's your flesh and blood and you have every right to want your son with you. I was just really hoping that we could work out an arrangement so that Jacob could still be around us and the kids as much as possible," Rene requested.

"Of course! Without a doubt," Tyrese responded. "I need you guys. I can't do this by myself. I know you love him and he loves you. I would never take him from you or stop you from seeing him. You're his family."

Rene promised herself that she wouldn't get emotional, but it wasn't working. Hearing Tyrese say that he understood that Jacob was family to them and that he would never keep Jacob away filled her heart and spirit with so much joy. The tears began to flow.

"Why are you crying?" asked Jalen, concerned.

"I'm. So. Happy!" Rene bellowed out, gasping for air after each word like a kid.

The three of them burst into laughter. After a little more small talk, they were able to collectively arrange a visitation schedule for Jacob and Tyrese. Since Jalen and Rene moved, they now were about forty-five minutes away from Tyrese. He agreed to drive to their house on Fridays to pick Jacob up so they could spend time together. Jalen agreed to meet Tyrese halfway on Sunday evenings to get Jacob.

"Okay, before we leave, I have two things that I really need you to be on board with," warned Rene.

"What might those be?" Tyrese asked.

"The first item is please, no matter what, if by chance Nina's mom and sisters reach out to you about seeing Jacob, tell them absolutely not. I don't trust them. They are too money hungry. Those dumb heffas might try to kidnap Jacob or something," explained Rene.

"Understood. I would never do that anyway," Tyrese assured her. "What's number two?"

"Even though Jacob will be staying with us, I am fully aware, and I completely understand that Jacob is your son. You can see him whenever you want. You can come get him whenever you want, just pretty please give us a heads-up. You know, just in case we have plans or something so we can make adjustments. We will of course do the same and keep you informed as well. Deal?" Rene offered.

"Fair enough. I have no problem with that. So, we good now, coparents?" Tyrese jokingly asked.

Rene and Jalen answered together in the midst of laughing, "We're good, baby daddy!"

Tyrese came to the house to spend time with Jacob a few times before he took him for an overnight visit. It did not take long for their bond to develop. Tyrese was a great dad. He even starting giving Rene and Jalen $350 every two weeks to help take care of Jalen. No matter how many times they told Tyrese he didn't have to give them anything, he insisted and would not take no for an answer.

Eventually, Jacob was spending every weekend with his dad. During the off-tax season, he would go for weeks at a time. Rene never took a dime of the money Tyrese gave them. She was secretly putting it all in a savings account for Jacob to use later in life. She still considered Jacob to be her own, and nothing was going to change that.

There were days when Rene missed her friend more than words could ever express. The last months of Nina's life were full of confusion and chaos, but the years before were full of laughter and good times. As bad as everything had gotten, the good memories that Rene had of Nina without a doubt outweighed the bad.

Rene never had a friend like Nina. As crazy, boisterous, outspoken, fearless, and ghetto as Nina was, her heart was ginormous. She was the epitome of loyal. That was hard to find in a person. She would have done anything for Rene, and Rene would have graciously returned the favor.

Nobody understood their friendship, and no one ever would. Sometimes in life, when you find someone who understands everything about you and can finish your sentence before you get the chance to, you couldn't care less about what other people think. All that matters is you and the relationship you share with your friend. Nina had some issues, there was no doubt about that, but at the end of the day, Rene knew that nobody would ever care for her the way Nina did.

Rene reflected on her marriage often as well. She loved Jalen, but it was hard to ignore that so much dishonesty and so many secrets had driven them apart and almost permanently ended the life they were trying to build together. All the times that Rene was unsure of Jalen's faithfulness and his commitment to their marriage turned out to be for no reason. In some respects, her husband wasn't the one with the mistress . . . she was.